Dreams were all she'd ever allowed for herself. Not out of uncertainty—she had always known that when the time was right she would willingly open that door and see what really lay on the other side—but because she was waiting for the right woman to come along.

She had spent most of her adult life looking forward to falling asleep more than to waking up, but now her dreams were stepping out of the darkness to wrap around her very much awake and aware body. The right woman was sitting next to her and she was ready for whatever might happen next.

Erotic Interludes

Volume 1

Edited by
M. Broughton Boone

2013
Cape Winds Press
Daytona Beach, FL

First Edition
ISBN 978-1-58972-007-7

Published by Cape Winds Press
http://www.CapeWindsPress.com

Cover art: *The Gates of Dawn*. 1900.
by Herbert Draper (1863-1920)

BOOKS BY THE AUTHORS

ALLERGIC REACTION (Leslie Adams)

BARNFIRE (Rebecca Montague)

A WILD SEA (Rebecca Montague)

TABLE OF CONTENTS

The Opening

Vicky Smythe

I wanted nothing so much as to taste her lips, and all the other parts of her. She was gorgeous in the way that only a lesbian with femme tendencies could be. Dark auburn hair fell in curly masses around her shoulders. Her hazel eyes betrayed a sense of humor that was echoed in the laughing tone of her voice; both charming and intriguing at the same time.

She wore no makeup and she didn't need it. We had only known each other an hour, and already I was so wet for her I couldn't stand myself. Her name was Christa, and while she hadn't captured my heart, she had certainly captured the part of me that wanted to take her somewhere private and fuck her until she exploded with the brilliant intensity of a camera's flash.

It wasn't as if we'd met in a bar where alcohol made lust easier to come by. We'd been introduced at the opening of my friend Susan's photography exhibit. She was a photographer as well, and when I asked what her specialty was she gave me an intimate smile and said black and whites. Realizing that she hadn't quite answered my question made her even more mysterious. I knew she was a lesbian from the way that Susan introduced us, making a point of mentioning that Christa was single and that we had a lot of things in common. That suited me fine because I wanted to get to know her better. A lot better.

I knew that she found me interesting as well from the way that she sought me out about ten minutes later, holding two glasses of wine.

"I noticed that your glass was empty, Patricia," she said with a secret smile, handing me one of them.

I accepted the wine, put my empty down on a nearby table and smiled back. "How thoughtful of you," I replied.

"Susan is doing quite well." She glanced around the room at the crowd and then returned a steady gaze to my face. "She should sell more than a few prints."

"She's becoming quite popular." I paused. "Do you exhibit?"

Christa laughed. "Sometimes, in select galleries. Not locally though."

"Why not?" The more she spoke the more curious I became.

"I'm very picky about who sees my work." Her eyes met mine. "I like women who appreciate the sensuality of them. I have a feeling that you would."

A tingling started in my groin. "So what exactly is it that you do?"

"Female nudes. My audience is almost exclusively lesbian." With her words, the tingling turned to throbbing.

"Then I'm sure I would love them."

"I'm glad Susan introduced us." She smiled invitingly. "She has a knack for knowing when people will get along well."

Thinking just how well I'd like to get along, I nodded. "I'm glad too. It isn't every day you meet someone so … intriguing."

"You intrigue me too," she replied. "Perhaps we'll have the chance to get to know each other better."

For the next hour, she stayed close by me, often touching my arm and giving me a private smile that increased my want for her every time I saw it. By the time we had made the circuit of the gallery, every nerve of my body was aware of the curve of her breasts and the hard points of her nipples that showed through the fabric of her blouse. I could feel the wetness between my legs and was sure that I would come instantly if her tongue touched my clit.

She was waiting for me when I came out of the bathroom a time later, her hand on the knob of a door that led off to the right of the hallway. The top button of her blouse was undone, revealing even more of her cleavage than it had before. I could just see the lace at the top of her bra. A surge of electricity hit my groin and my nipples began to ache. We studied one another for a scant moment before she spoke.

"Did I mention how much butch women turn me on?"

I grinned at her. "Lucky for me I'm butch."

She opened the door. "Lucky for both of us," she replied.

I followed her inside the room, closing and locking the door behind me. We were in an office, and a comfortable looking couch sat along one wall. Christa turned to me and unfastened another button on her blouse. I stepped forward, took her by the elbows and kissed her hard. She made a guttural sound in her throat as her lips parted.

My tongue delved into her mouth and danced against hers. Her hands slid around my waist and she stepped forward, pressing her body into me as she rocked forward slightly. I moved my hands to cup her ass, holding her hips against mine. She worked my shirt out of my pants and ran her fingers over the bare skin at the small of my back. We kissed hotly and then I moved my lips to her neck, biting against it as she groaned.

"I've been wet for you for an hour," she said in a breathless voice. "When I saw you walk in I knew I had to have Susan introduce us."

I stepped away from her and moved my fingers to the buttons of her blouse. "You're the hottest woman here. I couldn't help but notice you." She put her hands on my shoulders as I unbuttoned her shirt. "I want to see you naked."

"I want you inside me," she replied. "I want you to fuck me."

"I plan to." Hearing her say the word sent a shudder of excitement through me. I slid her blouse off her shoulders and she dropped her arms and shrugged out of it. Her bra was lacy and teasing, and the hardened points of her nipples pushed up against the fabric as if trying to tear through it. When I pulled the bra off, I could see that her firm breasts were as tanned as the rest of her body, her nipples dark pink rising from puckering brown circles.

I bent my head and captured a hardened nub between my teeth, feeling the tremor that passed through her body as I sucked it into my mouth. Her hand came to the back of my head and she pulled me forward against her breast. I let the nipple scrape between my teeth and then straightened up, capturing her nubs between thumb and forefinger as my mouth claimed hers again.

She shuddered as I rolled her nipples between my fingers. "Harder," she gasped.

Eagerly I complied, pinching as I pulled them away from her body and let them fall back between my fingers with a snapping motion. Finally, I took her hand and led her to the couch. I unfastened the buckle of her belt and then the button of her slacks. As I pulled them down, I saw that she wore neither hose nor underwear, the hair of her triangle thick and neatly trimmed.

She kicked off her pumps and stepped out of her slacks, standing naked before me, one hand on a jutted out hip and the other resting on the front of her thigh. Her expression beckoned as she slowly drew that hand up her belly and across a breast before crooking her finger and giving me a long, slow, seductive smile.

I stepped against her, sliding my hand between her thighs and finding the slick heat of her hunger. I put my other arm around her waist and held her as I slid two fingers into her center. She moaned and rocked forward against my hand. I drew out and pressed back in, and then slid my fingers over her hardened clit before bringing them to my mouth. Her juice was sweet; the taste increased my desire to run my tongue over and into the source of that wetness.

Her hands came to my chest, moving to unbutton my shirt. I allowed her to pull it off and then undid my bra myself. I could see the hunger in her eyes as she took in my breasts and the hardness of my nipples. I might be butch, but I take pride in my breasts, knowing what a turn on the slightly pendulous weight of them was to most women.

She reached out and circled her hands over both erect nubs before taking them between thumb and forefinger, pinching and slowly rolling them as a moan escaped my lips. I kicked off my shoes, undid my belt and my slacks and pushed them and my boxers down before taking her hands and sitting her down on the couch.

I sat beside her, turned and pressed her body down into the seat cushions as I came on top of her, sliding one leg between her thighs and pressing in against her heat. She opened her legs wider, putting one foot on the floor, and slid her arms around my shoulders. I claimed her mouth again as I moved against her feeling her wetness on my thigh.

"Don't tease me," she begged when I lifted my mouth away. "I don't want to wait any longer."

"Then you won't."

I sat up on my knees and slipped my fingers once more into the tangle of her hair. My thumb moved across her rigid tip as I slid two fingers into her again. She groaned and tilted her hips back, making it easier for me to drive into her. Two fingers just didn't seem like enough so I added a third one, feeling her tremble as I filled her. A long 'yes' escaped her lips when I began to thrust into her hungry well.

I leaned forward to take a nipple between my fingers, pinching it as she begged me for more, harder, faster. She pulled her knees up to her chest, allowing me to push more deeply into her. Finally, I could feel the orgasm growing and led her to it as the walls of her center tightened, trying to capture my hand. She called out my name once, twice, three times, arching her back, her head turning side to side as the spasms overtook her.

Before she had completely come down, I withdrew my fingers and slid down her body, kneeling on the floor so that I could bury my face between her thighs. She cried out as my lips caught her clit, sucking it into my mouth and vibrating against it with my tongue. I lapped the length of her, enjoying the taste of her juices and the way her hips ground against the cushions as I reclaimed her hardened tip. Very shortly, she arched her back again and blew into an even stronger orgasm.

I let her catch her breath before moving up her body and straddling her shoulders. She looked at me with hunger, put her hands on my hips and pulled me down, capturing me with her mouth. I felt her tongue slide into the source of my wetness and then move firmly up to my clit. She was an expert with her mouth, and soon had me writhing against her face as I came. Her tongue danced against me until I reached down and pressed my hand against her forehead, pulling away from her lips.

I slid off the couch and knelt on the floor, resting my head on her chest and breathing raggedly.

Finally, she spoke. "God, you're good."

I turned my head and a bit against the curve of her breast. "You make it easy," I replied. "You're unbelievably hot."

I leaned back and she sat up, running a hand through her hair. "Do I look like I just got fucked silly?"

"No."

She smiled. "We really should get back." We got dressed in silence. As I went to unlock the door, she put one hand against my cheek and kissed me softly. "Thank you. That was a lot of fun."

"For me too."

We stepped into the hall. Christa glanced toward the gallery and then turned toward the bathroom. "You go ahead. I want to make sure I look OK."

I ran a quick hand through my hair and went back to the reception where Susan caught my eye and gave me a knowing grin. I worked my way through the crowd to her side.

"It looks like the two of you hit it off." Her voice danced with laughter.

"Yes, we did," I said, still feeling a little breathless.

"I thought you would."

After thanking her for introducing us, I went outside for a smoke. When I came back in, Theresa was nowhere to be found. The crowd was thinning considerably, and I wondered where she'd gotten to.

A few minutes later, Susan came up to me. "She left. She said to thank you for a wonderful time."

Strangely, I was a little disappointed, even though I'd only intended what happened as a quick interlude. I had at least hoped to say goodbye. Susan was studying me.

"I wouldn't mind running into her again," I replied more lightly than I felt. "She certainly made things interesting." I paused. "I suppose I should be going too. It's getting late."

"And I'm sure you need to clean up." Susan laughed when I blushed.

"Yes I do, actually." I turned to go but Susan reached out and touched my arm.

"Christa asked me to give you this." She pressed something into my hand.

It was a business card with the name Christa Montgomery on it. I turned it over. On the back, in neat handwriting, were a telephone number and the words 'call me'. I smiled and tucked the card into my pocket, intending to do just that.

EMERALD EYES

Leslie Adams

It was a humid summer evening, the air thick and sticky as only a summer night in the south can be. In the distance, an occasional rumble of thunder announced the passage of a storm, but by the lake only the katydids and the pounding of Stephanie's heart broke the silence.

She knew that Beth, though sitting right next to her, couldn't hear the thudding in her chest, but she could and she didn't know what to make of it. She didn't know why her pulse was racing, why her stomach was aflutter, or why she could feel Beth's heat so distinctly. She didn't know, but sensed that she would soon find out.

They sat on top of a picnic bench, thighs just touching. Beth was leaning back on her hands, but Stephanie sat stiffly upright, trying to decide if she should suggest they get back in the canoe and return to the camp. There had been nothing in Beth's tone when she asked if Stephanie wanted to pause at the picnic area, and Stephanie had assumed Beth wanted to smoke, something forbidden back at the church campground.

But Beth hadn't smoked; now they sat silently looking out over the water, and Stephanie couldn't figure out why she didn't want to leave. Beth shifted, sitting back up, one arm a stripe of fire against Stephanie's back.

"Dinner was good," Beth said offhandedly. "Did you like your trout?"

"Yes. We could have stayed for dessert, though. I wouldn't have minded." When Beth suggested they leave the inn without looking at the sweets menu, Stephanie had assumed she was trying to be considerate of Stephanie's earlier voiced concern about calories and her weight. Now, she wasn't sure.

Beth's smile seemed secretive, and her emerald green eyes sparkled as she looked at Stephanie and laughed. "I had another idea for dessert."

"What?"

"Do you think Pastor John will notice if we're late getting back?" Beth glanced in the direction of the campground, half a mile down the lake and shrouded in darkness, and then back at Stephanie.

Stephanie blinked a few times at the change in subject. "How late do you think we'll be?"

"Depends." Beth shrugged. "Do you want to go back?"

Stephanie shook her head, even though she knew they ought to and that Pastor John would be very aware of their absence before much longer. She couldn't put a finger on it, but in all her twenty years, she had never wanted to be alone with someone as much as she wanted to be alone with Beth then.

"It's really muggy," she said. "I can't believe it's still this hot at nine o'clock."

"It could get hotter," Beth replied softly, looking deeply into Stephanie's eyes. "A lot hotter."

Stephanie tore her gaze from Beth's and tried to look at the lake. Her heart had started pounding even more, and she found herself keenly aware of Beth's presence so close beside her. She had thought Beth good looking when they first met, though it hadn't seemed to mean anything at the time. Beth *was* good looking; tall, muscular, with a ready grin and a way with words that somehow drew Stephanie in.

Now, three weeks later, Beth's attractiveness had taken on an unfamiliar and somewhat discomforting sharpness. Stephanie looked back at her companion and started to wonder why exactly they had stopped where they were. There was enough of a moon that she could see Beth's chest rising and falling, and realized with acute embarrassment that her mind was imagining that chest devoid of its covering shirt.

This isn't right, Stephanie thought. *I shouldn't be feeling like this. I shouldn't want....*

"Are you ok?" Beth turned, put her free arm across Stephanie's lap and smiled again. "You look a little strange."

"I...." Stephanie's throat was dry. "I feel a little strange," she admitted.

Beth's gaze searched her face. "Strange good? Or strange bad?"

Stephanie asked herself the same question, and was shocked at the answer. She glanced away, and then back. Beth's face was very close to hers. "I'm not sure."

"Let's find out, shall we?" Beth's voice was a whisper, her expression suddenly serious.

Stephanie started to speak and couldn't, could only stare back at Beth and hold her breath waiting for what would happen next. She waited only a moment before Beth leaned in and kissed her. The explosion of fire that shot through her body as she felt Beth's lips on hers drew a groan from deep within. She wanted to push Beth away, wanted to pull her closer, wanted to run but knew she would stay.

The kiss deepened as Beth brought her arms around Stephanie's torso and pulled her closer. Stephanie's mind spun as her body responded in way she couldn't understand. After an eternity, or perhaps a few seconds, she felt Beth's tongue tracing her lips, seeking to part them and slip into her mouth. As she allowed her in, she knew she was surrendering more than a kiss to the woman who held her.

The touch of Beth's tongue against hers sent another wave of liquid fire through her body. She shuddered, wondering how it was possible to want so desperately to draw another in. Her mind touched briefly on the fact that they were not too far from the church camp, from a physical reminder that what they were doing shouldn't be happening, and then Beth's hands moved into her hair and she lost all coherent thought.

Finally, Beth pulled back, leaving Stephanie gasping for breath. She studied Stephanie's face for a moment before smiling, nervously this time it seemed.

"Are you still ok?" she asked quietly.

Swallowing hard, Stephanie nodded. "I shouldn't be. I know I shouldn't be. But...." She trailed off as the need for Beth's mouth rose and overwhelmed her. Beth made a startled sound as Stephanie kissed her, and then another that could have been a purr before their tongues danced again.

Beth's hands moved across her back, down to her waist, and slipped under Stephanie's t-shirt. Her fingers were red hot coals wherever they touched Stephanie's skin; her hands traced up Stephanie's spine, lifting the shirt as they went. Stephanie found herself needing to feel the same parts of Beth, and soon they were both topless, shirts and bras discarded in a flurry of hunger.

"I've wanted to see you like this since we met," Beth said in a voice thick with desire. Her fingers followed the lines of Stephanie's neck, shoulders, the hollow of her throat, and then down to the curve of breasts that no one but Stephanie herself had ever touched.

Stephanie groaned again when those gentle, soft fingers began circling inward, brushing lightly across her hardened, aching nipples. She arched her back against Beth's hands, wanting more and not sure what more would mean. Beth, too, groaned and pushed her back until she lay on the picnic table looking up into hungry, eager eyes.

It was only a breath before Beth bent her head, her lips following the path her fingers had taken. As they closed around one nipple, Stephanie let out a little shriek of pleasure that faded into a long moan when Beth's tongue began to dance against her.

"Oh, God—" Stephanie gasped, finding Beth's shoulders with her hands and then moved to the back of her head, holding her against her chest. Beth moved her mouth to the other breast, her fingers capturing the one she had left. Stephanie gasped again and felt a dart of electricity race down and explode between her thighs.

Beth kissed her way back to Stephanie's mouth and lifted away, looking down at her. "I want more of you. I want much more."

Stephanie shuddered. "Anything," she whispered. "Everything." Her fingers found Beth's breasts, the feel of her rigid nipples a sensation she knew would remain with her forever. Beth arched toward her, slipping a hand behind her head and lifting her. Stephanie tasted sweat and heat, finally drawing a nipple into her mouth in a searing moment of hunger that almost staggered her ability to comprehend.

She reached up to pull Beth against her mouth, but Beth

resisted. Before Stephanie could protest, she felt Beth's hands at the button of her jeans. With agonizing slowness, Beth unzipped her pants and pulled them down. Stephanie lifted her hips automatically, feeling the air on her thighs and then—suddenly—Beth's breath against the cotton of her briefs.

"Beth ... dear Lord...."

Beth turned her head, nipping lightly at the tender inside of Stephanie's thigh. Her fingers brushed across the fabric covering Stephanie's now pulsing center, pressing in ever so slightly against the wetness that was soaking through. Stephanie shuddered, knowing now what Beth wanted, and wanting nothing more herself than to surrender it to her.

"You smell so good," Beth murmured, her voice partially muffled. She pushed at Stephanie's jeans, sliding them further down.

Stephanie kicked off her tennis shoes and allowed Beth to pull her pants completely off, and then bit her lip against another surge of wetness as she felt Beth's fingers slip under the band of her briefs. They, too, slipped down her legs and ended up on the ground, leaving Stephanie naked and shivering with anticipation.

Beth ran her hands up the insides of Stephanie's thighs, her thumbs pressing just at the edges of the mound at their join. Stephanie closed her eyes, willing Beth to move further in. She felt fingers sliding through her hair, pressing against the swollen wetness of her center. Beth began to explore her, her fingers slipping between Stephanie's lips, sliding upward against the hardened button of Stephanie's clit in a steady rhythm.

"Please. Beth, please." Stephanie spread her legs wider, shocked at her urgent need to feel more than Beth's fingers.

When Beth dropped her head and burrowed her tongue into the wetness, Stephanie screamed. Her scream tangled off as the sensations began to swirl within her, Beth's tongue—soft against her, then hard, slipping inside the source of her wetness, and then again soft—drawing feelings Stephanie had never experienced out of the depths and into the night.

Beth shifted so that Stephanie's thighs rested on her shoulders, her hands moving up to claim Stephanie's nipples. Stephanie arched her back again, her own hands clawing at the table, tangling into Beth's hair as she felt the pulsing, liquid hunger in her belly growing, flooding her body, and finally bursting into a spasming ecstasy that tore a scream from her that echoed against the forest around them.

As the waves of pleasure slowly faded, Beth moved up her body once again, now kissing her with her face wet from Stephanie's orgasm. Stephanie tasted herself on Beth's lips and felt one more sharp spasm take her. She felt Beth's heart pounding against her, and allowed the desire for Beth's body to overtake her.

She felt clumsy as she reached to undo Beth's pants, but Beth helped her and soon it was Beth who lay on her back and Stephanie who tasted her skin as she moved from her neck to her breasts, and then further down. She breathed in the musky scent of Beth's need, covered her fingers with wetness, and began to move against her. Beth's hips caught her rhythm and she began to moan. The feeling of control that swept through Stephanie's body startled her, as did the desire, quickly fulfilled, of feeling Beth from inside.

As her fingers slipped into Beth's well, Beth drew in a sharp gasp and grabbed at her shoulders. Stephanie paused.

"No?"

"Yes. Oh ... please ... yes...." Beth's voice was ragged.

Stephanie slowly buried her fingers, feeling Beth

shuddering, and then pulled back before again pressing in. Beth's groaned, "Oh God" sent a shiver of wicked pleasure through Stephanie's body, and she dropped her head against Beth's wetness with shocking eagerness, seeking out the swollen nubbin that she so wanted as her fingers delved again and again into Beth's heat.

The taste of Beth's body was unfamiliar and yet as satisfying as a cup of hot cocoa on a cold winters' day. Stephanie savored the erratic movement of Beth's hips, the moaning pleas—*harder ... there ... please ... God. Oh. GodohgodohGOD ... Stephanie!*—and as Beth blew into orgasm, the pulsating spasms that closed around her fingers and the rush of wetness from deep within. She held against Beth until her writhing had stilled and then moved back beside her.

They lay side by side, panting, for a long silent time. Finally, Beth rolled over and rose on an elbow, smiling down at Stephanie. Stephanie smiled back.

"Are you still ok?"

Stephanie laughed. "I'm not sure I've ever been so much more than ok."

"You have no idea how much I've wanted you." Beth traced a line down Stephanie's cheek with her free hand, moving across her lips before tapping her on the nose. "I was terrified."

"You? Terrified? Of what?"

With a sigh, Beth sat up and drew her knees to her chest, wrapping her arms around them. "You. What if I was wrong—what if you said no?"

Stephanie sat up as well. "I knew there something about you from the first. I just didn't know what."

"Was that the first with a woman?"

"It was the first with anyone." Stephanie drew in a deep

breath.

Beth made a noise. "It was? I didn't think...."

"I always assumed I would wait for my wedding night but— "

"Oh, I'm so sorry," Beth interjected. "I'm sorry I— "

Stephanie lifted her hand and touched Beth's lips, silencing her. "I'm glad I waited. I'm glad I waited for this ... for you. I never wanted to marry; now I know why." She looked away. "Pastor John is going to have a coronary when we get back."

Beth was silent for a long moment, staring at the ground. Finally, she lifted her gaze to Stephanie, her expression tentative. "So you don't think we're going to Hell?"

"Hell was wondering what was wrong with me. Hell was thinking I had no choice but marriage and what came with it." Stephanie smiled softly. "No, I don't think we're going to Hell; I think we're being saved from it. Even if we're never together again, I think we've been saved."

"I'd like to be with you again." Beth touched Stephanie's face.

"I'd like that too. One more kiss though, and we should get back."

Beth curled her lips into a smile. "Just one kiss?"

"Maybe two." Stephanie smiled back. "But no more."

It was nearly midnight before they beached their canoe back at the campground. As they had suspected, Pastor John was waiting for them.

"Where have you two been?" he demanded, arms crossed. "Not drinking at the inn, I hope."

The two women exchanged glances. "No, Pastor John, we haven't been drinking," Stephanie said. "We were ... discussing heaven. Time got away from us, I guess."

The pastor looked between them before snorting. "Well

that's all fine, but you shouldn't be out on the lake so late."

"We won't be," Beth promised, glancing at Stephanie with a private smile. "Will we, Sister Stephanie?"

"No, Sister Beth, we won't."

"To bed with both of you," Pastor John ordered. "We have a sunrise service tomorrow."

The pair nodded and moved toward the row of cabins where their fellow campers lay asleep. As they drew up to the one that Stephanie was staying in, Beth touched her hand.

"We will discuss heaven again, won't we?"

Stephanie's heart nearly burst at the hope and desire in Beth's voice. "Indeed, many more times I think."

They parted ways, and Stephanie crawled into bed with the knowledge that all of her questions had been answered by the joy in a pair of emerald eyes.

THE F-WORD

Rebecca Montague

Alyson's home. I hear the garage door open, followed by the slamming of her car door. I turn off the computer monitor and push the chair back. It's been five long days since I held her and I don't want to waste a second. There's been a hot wet ache in my cunt since I got off the phone with her two hours ago that playing a computer game has done nothing to calm. In all my twenty-eight years, I've never been so unendingly hot for a lover. Even after almost thirty months, the thought of her naked sends chills through me.

I pause by the hall mirror to make sure I look all right. Alyson says she loves my blonde hair super-short, so that's how I wear it, spiked up on top. I got it done this morning in anticipation of her coming home. My face is tanned from being outdoors all day. She prefers my green eyes without 'spectacles', as she calls them, so I've left my glasses by the computer. For a moment, I consider that my t-shirt, advertising our favorite beachside restaurant, is too casual, but it's too late to change it.

She's wearing her business suit, short skirt and fitted jacket, a soft blouse closed at the neck with that fluffy tie-like thing I'm always teasing her about. She's carrying her briefcase, but no bags; she must have left them in the car. That, and the look on her face, tells me she's missed me as much as I did her.

She's in my arms as soon as she gets through the door, briefcase hitting the floor by her feet. I kiss her hard the first time, just to feel her lips. The second time I'm a little gentler, but not much. Her mouth opens under mine and I taste her tongue. Her hands slip into the back pockets of my jeans.

"How was the drive?" I ask after a minute or two as I help her out of her jacket. Or at least, slide it off her shoulders. Her hands are still in my pockets.

"Long," she responds, pulling her hands out of my pockets and running her fingers up my back. She shrugs her coat off in one graceful motion and drapes it over one of the kitchen chairs with that preciseness of hers, folded in neatly in half. She runs a hand through her long auburn hair, and smiles at me. "It always is when I'm coming home."

"Do you want something to drink?" I reach up and grab one end of the silky tie-thing and pull. The knot unravels and it slides from around her neck. I consider using it later but decide against it; she'd kill me if I got it wrinkled.

"Only your ambrosia, dearest." Alyson has a way with words. I didn't even know what ambrosia was until we met. "I've been thinking about it for an hour."

"Just an hour?" I lean against the kitchen counter and cross my arms, grinning at her. "Got lost in the audio course, I guess." She's forever buying these lectures on CD for her road trips. The current one is on the Ethics of Aristotle. When it had arrived in the mail, I'd asked her why anyone would care about the ethics of some dead Greek guy. She'd screwed up that cute little nose of hers and informed me that it was a book, *Nichomachean Ethics*. I knew that, but it's fun to tease her.

Alyson gives me that 'you're being evil' look that makes me melt. "I got distracted talking to you on the phone. But it's a little difficult driving through rush hour traffic in Jacksonville while thinking about the abounding joys waiting at home."

"So now I'm a distraction?"

She walks very slowly over to me and puts one hand on the counter on either side of me and kisses me, not quite hard, but close. "You, my dear, are as distracting as sunset in the Keys." Considering just how amazing sunset in Key West can be, I'm pretty pleased with her comment. "Whenever I'm coming home from a trip, the only thing I can think about for the last fifty miles is making love with you. That's agony enough."

"Well, I'd hate to keep you waiting any longer than that." My fingers are on the buttons of her blouse, but she stops me and takes my hand. I let her lead me into the bedroom.

She pushes the door closed and leans against it, grinning. She lifts her hand and crooks a finger at me. "Come here, little girl."

I growl and move against her, pushing her into the wood of the door frame with my body; finding her neck with my teeth. She draws in a sharp breath and grabs the back of my head. I pull back from her just enough to fit my hands between our bodies, unbutton her blouse, and claim her breasts over her bra, my mouth finding hers. She groans around our kiss as I press into her again, my hips fitting with hers. I'm as wet for her right now as I was the first time I took her.

It takes only a few moments to move her to the bed, stripping her as I go. She kicks off her shoes and wiggles out of her hose, which are damp at the crotch. She's not wearing anything under them. I push her across the mattress and look down as she arranges herself against the pillows. She looks up at me with an innocent expression.

"So, my strong Amazon; whatever do you intend to do with me?"

I pull my t-shirt off and unfasten my jeans as quickly as I can. Bra and boxers hit the floor and I kneel next to her on the mattress. "I'm going to make you scream." I don't have her vocabulary and I can't describe my intentions in flowery phrases. I just know I'm going to fuck her. Fuck her hard and long, until she rips the sheets off the bed and begs me to stop.

She folds her arms behind her head. "Ravish away, Dusty."

I bend over and suck one of her nipples into my mouth, vibrating against it with my tongue. My fingers claim the other one, pinching and rolling. She moans and grasps the pillow with both hands, arching her back against my lips. I move on top of her, sliding one leg between her thighs, switching my mouth to the other tit. Her pubic hair is wet and scratchy against my skin.

I move my hand down and slip into the wetness, finding her swollen and hot. Her clit is a hard button for my fingers to tease. I know she wants me inside her, but I'm going to make her wait; her clit interests me much more at the moment. I put a finger firmly on it and roll in a small circle. Her hips jerk. I let my fingers wander over her, making long slow strokes from cunt to clit, teasing at her entrance before moving away.

"God, Dusty, please…."

"Please, what?" I look into her blue eyes. They are shining with need.

"Take me."

I smile at her, feeling slightly evil. All her fancy words vanish when it comes right down to what she likes to call 'brass tacks.' Not even Alyson can call it making love when she's drowning in the hot, sticky need of it.

"I am taking you." I flick a finger firmly across her clit.

She shudders. "You're a tease."

"Tell me." I position my fingers at her sucking hole and press ever so slightly. "Say it." She hesitates and I start to move my hand. "Then you aren't ready."

"Fuck me." The words slip from between her cultured lips with an ease that would probably shock everyone in her office. "Fuck me hard."

I reward her by sliding two fingers into her, feeling her slick walls grasping, pulling me in. I press as far as I can before pulling almost out and then slamming my hand back against her. She bucks up from the bed, pushing against me, trying to take me even further in. I add a third finger. She moans her pleasure, spreading her legs wide. The only part of me touching her is my hand, and I fuck her hard, slowing at times to prolong the pleasure, then speeding up to match the lifting of her hips.

After the third tiny orgasm ripples through her body, I know that she's teetering on the edge of violent explosion, and I know exactly what she wants me to do to push her over. I slide down on the bed and capture her clit with my mouth. As I suck the swollen tip between my lips, Alyson makes an unintelligible noise and grabs my head with both hands. I scrape her clit with my teeth and beat against it with my tongue, my hand continuing its in and out motion.

"Oh. God. Dusty!" She lets go of me and as I glance up her body, I see her grabbing for the headboard. Her fingers scratch along the surface and then she drops her arms and claws at the bottom sheet.

I slow my hand and make lapping strokes with my tongue from hole to clit, sensing the energy building inside her. She wiggles impatiently under me at the change of pace, but I keep at it for a bit longer before building back up to the hard, thrusting rhythm I know she loves. I suck her clit back into my mouth and use my tongue to pull the scream from her throat.

I feel the final orgasm take her, feel the walls of her cunt spasm, trying to capture my fingers. Her muscles are very strong and I know that my movements are causing even more intense waves as I keep thrusting into her, my tongue merciless against her clit. After what seems like an eternity, she clenches her legs tight against my ears.

"Stop," she gasps. I comply, leaving my fingers inside, and move on top of her. I kiss her dry lips and stroke her hair, feeling tiny tremors running through her body. One corner of the fitted sheet is off the mattress and half the pillows are on the floor. We lay in silence for a few minutes. I finally slip my hand from between her legs and lift it to suck the juices from my fingers. She watches me with a small smile. "Proud of yourself?" Her voice is teasing.

"Very," I reply. "Not bad for a warm-up."

She rolls me over onto my back and slides half on top of me. "No one has ever made me come as hard as you do. No one."

"That's because no one ever fucked you before."

"I hate that word," she says, screwing up her face.

I wrap my arms around her. I won't remind her that she used it twice. I never do. "Maybe so, but you sure like receiving it. It's the only time you ever really let go."

She buries her face against my neck and I smile to myself, knowing she's embarrassed. "I don't mean to be a prude." Her voice is muffled.

"You aren't. You're my genteel Southern lady. I'm your backwoods ruffian, and I'm going to do all those things to you that would make your society friends blush."

She looks into my face. "I love you, Dusty."

"Prove it. You've got one horny hillbilly underneath you. What do you plan to do about it?" I waggle my eyebrows at her and she laughs.

"Everything I can," she replies.

"Even the F-word?"

She slides her hand between my legs. "Especially the F-word."

Dream's Door

Leslie Adams

The flicker of the campfire and the sounds of laughter were far enough away that Toni could almost believe she was alone with Kara in the middle of the forest. They had walked for some distance along the lakeshore, and now sat staring up at the moon and the scattering of stars.

"You know why I wanted to take a walk," Kara said quietly, her face looking ethereal in the glow of the moonlight.

"Yes." Toni swallowed with anticipation. She'd wanted to take a walk for the same reason, only Kara knew her way around a woman's body and Toni had yet to learn.

They'd met that Friday when the group first gathered at the campground. Toni had come with a friend who thought she needed to get out of her shell and meet new people. Kara had arrived alone, though it became increasingly clear as the day wore on she didn't intend to stay alone all weekend, and equally clear that she thought Toni was just the one to keep her company.

Toni tended to be shy, but Kara's attention was hardly unwelcomed; in fact, Toni thought Kara was the hottest thing she'd seen in a very long time. Her friend's well-intentioned warning that Kara was into women and known for moving fast had only increased Toni's interest and heightened her awareness of Kara's physical attributes. She had long legs, an ample chest, and black hair that fell around her shoulders in ebon curls. She was exactly the sort of woman Toni dreamed about.

Dreams were all she'd ever allowed for herself. Not out of uncertainty—she had always known that when the time was right she would willingly open that door and see what really lay on the other side—but because she was waiting for the right woman to come along.

She had spent most of her adult life looking forward to falling asleep more than to waking up, but now her dreams were stepping out of the darkness to wrap around her very much awake and aware body. The right woman was sitting next to her and she was ready for whatever might happen next.

She wasn't sure how Kara had figured out she wouldn't reject an advance, but the question had come easily some time earlier; *would you like to take a stroll after dark?*

"Are you nervous?" Kara leaned toward her, eyes almost glowing.

Toni shook her head. "No. I thought I would be, but...."

"Good." Kara smiled. "You've never done this before, have you?" She didn't phrase it as a question, and didn't wait for an answer.

Before Toni could speak, Kara's mouth sought hers in a slow, simmering kiss, her hands coming to cup Toni's cheeks as she pressed her tongue with gentle insistence between Toni's willingly parting lips. The touch of that warm, soft tongue against her own sent an explosion of energy arcing through Toni's body; she groaned. Kara smiled against her and moved her hands into Toni's hair. They kissed again, this time with greater hunger. Kara reached down and started pulling Toni's t-shirt up.

The air on her body was cool, and Kara wasted little time stripping the rest of her clothes off, slipping out of her own before coming back to press Toni down onto the blanket they had laid out to sit on. Toni felt the heat growing as they touched skin to skin, and surrendered willingly when Kara sought out a nipple with her mouth.

As the raven haired beauty ran lines of molten heat across her breasts, Toni allowed her own hands at last to explore the curves of another woman's body, tracing her fingers down Kara's spine, across the curves of her ass, and back up her sides to her shoulders.

"You really want this, don't you?" Kara's voice was low and sultry, her words sending a rush of moisture to Toni's already hungry center.

"Yes," she gasped, and gasped louder when Kara slid easily down her body and spread her legs, dropping her face between her thighs and finding Toni's wetness with her mouth. "Oh, God...."

Kara's tongue explored the folds and valleys of Toni's heat, delving deeply into her grasping well before slipping up to dance against the rigid button of Toni's clit. Toni lifted against her, tangling her fingers into the woman's hair. "Please, Kara, please...."

Kara continued to move her tongue, first softly, then harder, and then soft melting heat again before she finally drew Toni's throbbing clit into her mouth and bit against it lightly, her tongue now pummeling the tip as her hands found Toni's nipples.

Toni felt the orgasm growing—the building pressure greater than anything she had ever experienced—and pleaded with Kara to send her over the edge. A few moments later, Kara complied, holding to her as she bucked and writhed, desperately trying to swallow the screams that rose from within the depths of the climax.

After it was done, Kara came beside her and grinned. "Did you like that?"

Unable to speak yet, Toni just nodded, and then tentatively reached to trace her fingers around Kara's nipples. Kara's grin turned hungry, and she moved again to position one breast at Toni's mouth. Toni tasted her skin, drew the nipple into her mouth and suckled at it, feeling Kara shudder.

She wondered for a moment what Kara might want of her, a question quickly answered as Kara slid up and straddled her shoulders, looking into her eyes with hungry intensity.

"Show me how much you liked it," she ordered as she lowered herself against Toni's face. Toni burrowed into the tangle of dark curls eagerly, seeking out the source of the wetness with her mouth, exploring with her tongue until she found Kara's own hardened clit.

Kara obviously liked what she was doing, arching her back with groaning pleas for more. She came suddenly and violently, and after she was done, she rolled away and sat up, looking at Toni with a heaving chest. "Like your first lesson in fucking a woman?" Her voice was slightly uneven as she fought for breath.

Toni considered the question briefly. The tastes, the feel, the scent of a woman were more satisfying than she'd dreamed they might be. There was one thing she still wanted to experience, though.

"I like what I've tried so far," she replied, her fingers working up Kara's thighs. "But I haven't actually fucked you yet."

Kara grinned at her. "We can fix that."

By the time they managed to pull their clothes back on, the campsite had gone silent and the fire no longer burned visibly. Walking back along the shore, Kara squeezed Toni's hand and whispered, "Care to schedule another lesson?"

"I can't wait," Toni responded. "Tomorrow?"

Kara grinned at her. "Sounds nice. Not enough time to spend with a woman as hot as you, but...."

"Do you make house calls?" Toni's heart started beating faster at the thought of having all night to spend entwined with the woman beside her.

"If the pay is right."

"Is getting tongued 'til you beg for mercy adequate pay?" Toni felt wanton and playful, the warm heat of afterglow still wrapped around her thoughts and the desire to hear Kara begging for mercy over-riding her usual quiet reticence in expressing herself.

Kara shuddered beside her. "I have an opening Sunday night." Her voice betrayed how hot she still was, pleasing Toni even more.

"I'll give you my address."

They got back to camp and crawled into their own tents after a brief but passionate kiss. As Toni drifted off, she realized that for once she was far more satisfied with remembering what had happened during the day than thinking about what might happen while she slept. She had opened the door to her dreams and found Kara on the other side, and dreams would never again be as good as the reality of a woman's kiss.

HORIZONTAL THERAPY

Vicky Smythe

This isn't a story about sex. It's supposed to be—and I like to write about sex. I can't recall a single story I've ever written that wasn't about sex on some level. But writing about sex requires me to be very *there*, and *there* I'm not. I haven't been since Sarah left.

So here I am, sitting in this god-awful retreat trying to write. I used to love writer's retreats, especially the ones my friend Kerry holds here at Falling Rainbow Ranch, but this has to be the most out-of-my-mind bored I've been in a long time. Worse, the session this afternoon is on writing sex.

Originally, Kerry wanted me to lead the class. After all, I have the reputation for writing some of the steamiest lesbian love scenes in print. I told her I couldn't, that I was off my game. She pouted and batted her eyes and tried to ply me with wine, but I didn't budge. That was Monday, four days ago. I should have taken her wine and kept drinking it, because this week is turning into a wasted trip.

The mix of women at Kerry's retreats used to fascinate me. Published authors, like me, sitting next to neophyte writers who just figured out last month that pen and paper could produce a story. I suspect some of them just come to rub elbows with their idols, maybe try and tip a famous dyke's heels into bed. I was as surprised as Sarah when I was first published to find out there were lesbian romance groupies. Who'd have figured?

Anyway, back to the story. Our assignment is to write a scene about two women exploring each other for the first time. Kids' stuff. I've done that scene a half dozen times through the years. Problem is, I haven't explored a woman for the first time since 2002, and my memory ain't what it used to be. Besides, dredging up how Sarah felt that first time isn't on my list of top ten things to do. At the moment, it falls somewhere between changing the litter box and trying to figure out just what that foil in the back of the fridge is supposed to contain.

I'm not saying Sarah was my muse, because she wasn't. I'm just not in the mood to be writing about hills and valleys of passion knowing hers are now under the exploration of Tina Gonzales. Go figure, she spends eleven years worrying about whether I'm dining "a la carte" with my fans, and she's the one who ends up doing take out.

I give up. I can't sit here and write this idiotic scene. This isn't high school, there's no reason I can't just get up and walk out.

* * *

The lake here is very peaceful. I figure a walk along the shore might sort me out, but I don't count on Kerry tracking me down. Kerry was very supportive through the whole breakup, and she's the one who pushed me to come this week. She's sort of a best friend, editor, and cheerleader all rolled into one; it was Kerry who got me started writing romance in the first place back in the 90's. But sometimes she's a bit overwhelming. This is looking like one of those times.

"Angelina, why'd you leave the session? I was looking forward to using your scene in the discussion." Kerry looks up at me with her wide chocolate eyes. I've always thought her eyes were great.

"Because there was no scene." I try not to sound as gruff as I feel. "I just couldn't do it."

"Look, woman, I know you can write a love scene. You've got to put Sarah out of your mind."

I stop walking and draw in a breath. I'm wondering whether she'll take it personally if I rip her head off. I settle for narrowing my eyes at her. "Three months ain't that long a time, Kerry. Not after all those years."

"No, it's not. But you still have to do it, and sulking isn't going to bring her back." Kerry puts her hands on her hips and stares right back at me.

I look at her hard. She's like a short, café au lait bulldog when she gets a thought in her head. "No, but it makes me feel better."

She rolls her eyes. "What you need is a good horizontal therapy session."

"Oh, and I suppose you're going to volunteer to be my therapist?" I have to laugh, even though I don't want to. Kerry's been celibate longer than I have, ever since her last girlfriend gave her the scare of her life by sharing needles with the unsavory crowd she was hanging out with at the time. So that makes it almost two years for Kerry. And she tells *me* I need to get over it.

Kerry crosses her arms under her breasts and gives me the once over. "If that's what it takes." I'm not expecting that. Kerry doesn't do white girls. She told me once we taste funny. Before I can figure out what to say back to her, she laughs. "Try not to miss the bonfire, would you?"

"Ok." It's the best I can manage. She pats my cheek and walks off. It takes me a while to decide she was kidding with me. She'd have to be. Even so, I feel thrown. I'm thinking now would be a good time to head back to my cabin for a drink.

* * *

The bonfire is a tradition at the Ranch. Friday and Saturday nights, everybody gets together and sits around the fire. Sometimes we talk, sometimes we sing. Sometimes there's improv storytelling. Tonight I don't participate much. I find staring into the flames more interesting. I do that, stare at fire. Sometimes I see stories. Now I just see Sarah leaving.

The night wears on and women wander off to bed. Finally, it's just Kerry and me. She's been quiet all evening too. I'm thinking it isn't like her, and I'm wondering why. She doesn't look at me, even though we're sitting on the same side of the fire.

We're silent for a long time. Finally, I glance over and see her eyes on me. The darkness seems to yield her unwillingly, and I watch the play of light and shadow across her face as the logs settle and the fire burns low. I think to myself how beautiful she is. I'm surprised by that; I've never really looked at her in that way before.

I feel like I need to say something. "I suppose it's time to turn in."

"If you're tired." Her voice is distant. "I don't think I can sleep right now."

"Why not?"

She looks at me levelly. I notice how full her lips are,

how the red-brown of them melts into the lighter brown of her face. "I've got a lot to think about."

"Anything I can help with?" I smile when she does, but hers fades quickly.

"You're the only one who could." She looks back at the fire. I see how smooth her skin is, like she's carved out of tan marble. The gray streaks in her short hair give her character, but her face hides its true age well. I find it hard to believe she's nearly forty-five.

"Well then, how?" I get a sense of inner turmoil from her. It bothers me. I don't like to see Kerry upset.

"I wasn't joking this afternoon." She doesn't face me as she says it.

My heart flips over and drops a fireball into my stomach. I try to sound light, but I'm afraid she'll hear my voice wavering. "About what, me needing to get laid or you offering to do it?"

"Both." She looks at me now. "It's killing me to see you so turned inward."

"Sex won't cure that."

"No, but it might start the healing." She drops her head and stares at her feet.

"It's pretty selfless of you to offer," I say, trying to puzzle out how to handle this. "I know how you feel about us white girls."

She stands and her eyes are fierce when she glares at me. "You don't know anything. And I didn't offer to be selfless."

I look up at her. "I had no idea—"

She interrupts me. "You weren't meant to. I wasn't about to come between you and Sarah. I guess it will always be about coming between you and Sarah though."

I watch her stride off. For a few seconds I just sit there, and then the little voice in the back of my brain kicks in and tells me to go after her. I do. I catch up with her at the bottom of the steps to her cabin. "Kerry...."

"What?" I'm not sure in the darkness, but I think she's crying. "What, Angelina? I'm sorry I told you. I shouldn't have presumed."

I kiss her. There's no intention; I just do it. Her lips are salty with tears. I kiss them away from her mouth and her cheeks. She doesn't try to stop me. "I'm sorry I was so flip. I just didn't see it coming."

"I've wanted you since we first met. Back then I was too hung up with the whole race thing to act on it, and then you met Sarah." Her voice is choked and she sniffles a couple of times.

"Let's go inside." I take her arm and start up the stairs.

She resists. "Don't come in if you're going to leave tonight."

I turn and look at her. I can barely see her face in the dim light from the window, but I know she's determined. I look inside myself; the ache I feel is growing, the ache to be with her. I don't want to be a jerk; I don't want to sleep with her just to make her feel better. And I realize it's the furthest thing from my mind. As I recognize my want for her, I wonder why I never saw it before.

She is still looking at me, waiting. I don't care about the why. All I care about is the want. "Let's go inside," I say again, "before I start undressing you here."

I explore her as I undress her. Her skin is silk under my fingers, her scent fills me with a deep aching need. I taste her mouth, her neck, her shoulder as I lower her to the bed. She pulls me on top of her, her hands studying the planes of my back and hips, her mouth hungry on mine.

I discover the fullness of her breasts with my fingers, and then with my lips. I drink in the taste of her, amazed at the subtle differences in each spot I kiss. Her scent fills my nose, also subtly changing as I move down her body. The gentle curve of her belly falls into the mass of curls between her thighs, and I learn her terrain with my mouth, feeling her arch under me.

I drink from her as she surrenders to me, drink both her wetness and the energy of her orgasm, riding her crest until she begs me, *no more*. And then I lie fully against her, take her in my arms, and kiss away the new tears that well up from her eyes as she thanks me.

She is tender with me, whispering her wonderment as she explores my body. I open to her, embracing her movements against me with a pleasure I thought I could never feel again, not sure I've ever felt. When she draws the final ounce of desire from me, I find myself crying with joy; joy that she loves me so well, and joy that I am fully hers.

I sleep at last, holding her close to my side as her scent continues to gently fill my dreams.

* * *

The next retreat comes, and I'm glad to volunteer to teach the session on writing sex. I've been prolific in the previous months, and Kerry's willing indulgence of my need for her keeps me filling the pages with tales of passionate love. I'm driven now, by the desire for her and the desire to put into words what I feel when I touch her.

I guess that this really is a story about sex. But I write this and think that no, it isn't, because sex is a superficial thing and what Kerry and I share is born deep within. This is a story about exploring hidden passion. This is a story about love.

GETTING TANGLED UP

Leslie Adams

"I need to get laid." Melissa tossed the TV remote onto the coffee table in disgust. "Three months is just too damn long."

It had been longer than three months, but she wasn't counting the two before her split with Jan. She'd really thought getting out of that disaster of a relationship would improve her sex life, but she'd found all-too-quickly that the friendly one-night stand was pretty much non-existent, and hanging out at the bar in hopes of getting lucky just didn't appeal any more.

Melissa leaned back and scowled at the ceiling. Why was it so hard for women to have an orgasm without getting their emotions all tangled up in it? She wasn't interested in another relationship, not yet—maybe not ever. The celibacy of being single was wearing extremely thin, however, and she was quickly descending into outright crankiness about it.

Finally, tired of dwelling on her frustration, she decided to head to the cigar store for a box of Lonsdales to restock her humidor. If she couldn't spend the night with a hot woman, she might as well spend it with a good smoke. She ran a brush through her short hair and spiked it up, noting that it was about time to bleach it again, threw on a t-shirt and jeans, and headed out to her truck.

There was only one other customer in the store when she stepped inside—surprisingly, another woman. She was perusing the selection of Cohibas and seemed very knowledgeable about what she was looking for. The owner of the shop glanced over and broke into a smile of recognition, waving to Melissa before returning to his customer. Melissa headed to the Arturo Fuentes and began looking for the Lonsdales.

"I'm surprised to see another woman in here." The woman's voice was smoky, matching her long brown hair and chocolate eyes. Melissa turned, a little startled.

"I was too."

"The Fuentes are a good smoke." She held a box of Cohiba Blacks and a torch lighter. "The Churchill got a good review in Cigar Aficionado."

"I prefer something a little smaller," Melissa replied, trying to keep her eyes off the brunette's cleavage, the curve of her breasts just showing in the V of her blouse.

"I'm more taken by taste than size."

Melissa was silent for a moment, sensing a hidden meaning in the woman's words. "It depends on the cigar, really."

"I'm Katherine."

"Melissa." The two shook hands. "You know a lot about cigars."

"It's one of my passions." Katherine smiled. "I like your haircut."

"Thank you." Again, Melissa had the feeling that there was something more to Katherine's words.

Katherine studied her for a moment before Melissa realized that she was looking pointedly at the rainbow necklace she wore. A wash of hunger came over her. Certainly, Katherine couldn't be a lesbian; that would be too much, too tempting.

"We should get together and compare notes on our favorite cigars," Katherine said unexpectedly. "It isn't every day I meet another woman who likes them."

Noting the slight hesitation in Katherine's voice merely increased the little ache between Melissa's legs. Being flirted with by a total stranger was exciting enough without the added fuel of unwanted celibacy; knowing how long it had been served only to stoke Melissa's desire into burning even brighter.

"That would be nice."

"Are you free this evening?"

Not expecting quite such a quick invitation, Melissa blurted out, "I'd love to."

Katherine smiled, a slow seductive smile that sent a shiver down Melissa's back. "Excellent. I'll make dinner."

They exchanged phone numbers and Melissa paid for her purchase, heading back to her truck with her heart pounding. She was almost certain that the evening would include more than talk about tobacco. That was fine with her; Katherine was just the sort of woman she went for, femme and forward. Melissa liked being seduced. It was a serious turn on.

After spending far more time than usual wondering what to wear to dinner, she finally settled on dressing casual butch; it would give the impression that she was approachable but still liked to be in control in bed. She was fairly certain that Katherine would be the aggressive one, but was willing to take charge if need be.

The directions Katherine gave when Melissa called later were easy to follow, and they chatted on the phone as Melissa drove the short distance to her apartment. It was on the second floor; she greeting Melissa at the door wearing a pair of slacks and a silk blouse unbuttoned far enough that her intentions were made very clear.

They talked about cigars over drinks and had a rather hurried dinner before retiring back to the living room with their wine. Melissa could tell Katherine was as eager as she was to get down to the real purpose for their meeting by the very visible and very hard points of the brunette's nipples rising beneath the softness of her blouse.

Conversation was short before Katherine leaned forward and looked directly into Melissa's eyes. "You know I didn't invite you here just to talk."

"I know," Melissa replied. "That's why I said yes."

Katherine's smile was the same seductive one from earlier in the day. "I thought we were on the same page." She got up and moved to sit beside Melissa on the couch. "I like the idea of stranger sex. Does it turn you on too?"

"Yes." Melissa's heart beat faster. The night was promising to be a lot of fun. "You've certainly got my interest piqued."

"Is that all I've piqued?" Katherine ran her fingers up Melissa's arm.

"No." Melissa felt her own nipples hardening as she spoke.

"Too few women are interested in sex for the sake of sex." The brunette paused to stroke Melissa's shoulder softly. "I find it much more enjoyable that way."

Melissa met her gaze with a smile. "So do I."

Katherine continued her movement up Melissa's neck to her ear, moving along it almost absently. "You're very good looking."

"You're gorgeous."

Their kiss was mutual. Katherine's tongue traced a line along Melissa's lips, insinuating itself inside her mouth with a gentle but insistent movement. The kiss grew deep and inside, as Katherine moved both hands up Melissa's arms to cup her face. Melissa felt the wetness growing between her thighs when Katherine pressed her down against the arm of the sofa and circled her waist with her arms, drawing her closer.

Katherine's teeth nipped lightly at Melissa's neck, then a bit harder. She worked a lazy line to Melissa's ear where she sucked her earlobe into her mouth and batted at it with her tongue before working her way back down to the hollow of Melissa's throat. Melissa spread her legs to allow Katherine to move her hips in between her thighs and felt the pressure in her groin growing when Katherine began a slow grind against her.

Melissa slid her hands between their bodies and found the rigid points of Katherine's nipples through the thin fabric of her blouse. Katherine let out a little groan. Melissa caught each hardened nub between thumb and forefinger and slowly rolled them back and forth before drawing them upward and letting them snap through her fingers. Katherine groaned a bit louder and sought her mouth once again.

They kissed for a few minutes longer before Katherine stood and held out her hand. Melissa took it and joined her, and Katherine led the way to the bedroom. She paused to press Melissa into the doorframe, her hands sure on the buttons of Melissa's shirt. They left a trail of shoes and clothing to the bed and fell across it together, bodies pressed against one another as their tongues battled in wet warmth.

Finally, Katherine lifted up and brought her hands to Melissa's belt. Melissa caught her breath as she unbuckled it and unfastened the button of her slacks. Her zipper came down easily, and she lifted her hips to allow Katherine to pull pants and boxers down past her thighs. She wiggled out of them and reached up to undo Katherine's slacks, sliding them down her legs. Katherine stood and Melissa watched as the fabric slipped off, puddling on the floor. She wore the scantest of thongs, and as Melissa watched, she slowly slipped them off revealing a cleanly shaved mons.

With a deliberate motion, she knelt on the bed between Melissa's legs. Sensually, she arched her body over Melissa's, her lips seeking a nipple, drawing it into her mouth as her tongue circled the tip in a slow, lazy motion. Melissa pressed upward against her face, a long moan escaping her lips. Katherine suckled at her breast, occasionally catching it between her teeth and scraping upwards. Her fingers sought out its sister to roll and pinch, drawing gasps of pleasure from Melissa. She switched breasts and Melissa felt the wetness increasing from her center. She brought her arms up around Katherine's chest and pulled her closer, feeling the points of her nipples pressing against her belly.

Katherine didn't pause very long before kissing her way down to the curly thatch of red hair at the termination of Melissa's thighs. She ran her tongue along the edge and down one thigh. She nibbled her way up the other one and then breathed hotly into the tangle of hair.

"You smell really good," Katherine commented. Without waiting for an answer, she dropped her head and buried her face against Melissa's center, her tongue burrowing between her lips to dip into the well of moisture that seemed to continuously flow from her. Melissa let out a loud groan and lifted her hips against Katherine's mouth.

Katherine's tongue explored her thoroughly, the peaks and valleys of her, before coming to rest against the swollen hardness of Melissa's clitoris. She vibrated against it, drawing moans of pleasure, then sucked it into her mouth and bit gently. The twinge of pain served only to increase the building pressure of gathering energy that meant Melissa was nearing the edge of orgasm. Katherine nursed on Melissa's rigid nub for several seconds before releasing it and moving back down to delve into Melissa's body, in short, sure strokes.

"God, please," Melissa begged. Katherine lifted her eyes and met Melissa's with a glinting look before returning to her clit to pummel against it with her tongue. Melissa arched her back—"Yes!"—the sensations spiraling outward into her nipples—"Katherine!"—before collapsing back into themselves in a violent, concentrated implosion of energy. The orgasm wracked her body as Katherine held to her, her tongue beating against her.

Finally, Melissa could take no more and pressed her hand against Katherine's forehead. Katherine slowed and stopped, her tongue pressed firmly against Melissa's clit. She flicked off it, drawing one more gasp from Melissa and lifted her head, a wicked grin wreathing her face.

"Oh. My. God." Melissa fought to catch her breath.

Katherine drew to her knees and moved up Melissa's body until they were facing one another. She dropped her head and kissed Melissa with a languid tongue, sending one more spasming shock through Melissa's body, and then rolled over to sit next to her.

"You come like a cannon," she observed, still smiling. "I'm going to have to wash the duvet."

"I don't think I've ever been tongued that well," Melissa

replied, rising onto her elbows. "You're amazing."

Katherine laughed. "Lots of practice. How much practice do you have?"

The thought of tasting Katherine's juices sent another shock through Melissa's body. "Enough, I think."

"Good." Katherine lay down on her back. "Ravish away."

She tasted as good as she looked, and Melissa drew impassioned gasps from her as she relentlessly lapped from the center of her heat to the hardened bud of her clit. She pressed against her with two fingers and Katherine gasped her assent, bucking up from the bed when Melissa slid into her. She groaned as Melissa's tongue resumed its assault while she simultaneously began to thrust against her with her hand

It seemed too soon for Melissa that she sensed the change in Katherine's movements. She tried to slow and prolong the pleasure, but Katherine was beyond it and blew into orgasm in spasms that clamped down on Melissa's fingers in repeating waves.

They held each other for a space of time before returning to their play, bringing one another to the heights of passion once, twice again before collapsing against the pillows, too exhausted to continue. There was a silence and then Katherine spoke.

"Would you like to stay the night?"

Melissa considered the invitation. "I think I should go home. I need to work in the morning."

Katherine didn't seem particularly disappointed. "Too bad; perhaps we could get together again. The discussion was fascinating and very pleasurable."

"I'd like that," Melissa replied, her body shivering with the anticipation of what another meeting might entail. "This weekend?"

"Of course."

Katherine stayed on the bed while Melissa dressed, then got up and reached for a robe.

"This was very enjoyable," Melissa said as they walked to the door.

"Indeed." Katherine leaned over and gave her a long, languid kiss that made Melissa wish that the weekend would come quickly. "Until this weekend?" Her eyes and her tone were eager.

"Until this weekend."

As Melissa drove away, she couldn't help smiling; she might not be ready to get emotionally involved again, but Katherine's eagerness—and expertise—promised a relationship she would certainly enjoy getting tangled up in.

A Woman Like Marty

Rebecca Montague

The snow was falling so thickly that I could hardly make out the lights of the house up ahead. It was the first I had seen in an hour, and I knew that I couldn't go on until morning. I pulled into the driveway of the small frame structure and prayed that the occupants would have pity on me.

If it hadn't been so damned important for me to be at that conference the next day I would never have attempted to drive back from the lake in a storm anyway, but my boss had made it clear that since I was the one who had pitched the account, I had to be the one to explain the fine print to the customer. Not only that, but things hadn't gone as I had hoped between me and Jack, so I was driving back irritated and wondering what was wrong with me.

Muttering curses under my breath, I slammed the car door, struggled through the snow to the porch of the house and knocked, then held my breath. A few moments passed before the door opened and I found myself faced with a tall, handsome, broad-shouldered red-haired woman of perhaps thirty-five. I caught my breath. Something about her tugged at me.

"Yes?"

"I'm sorry, I...."

She peered past me at my car and then took my by the arm and pulled me inside, closing the door behind me. "Only a damned fool would be driving a sports car in weather like this," she said, indicating the sofa. "You must be one of those lake people."

I nodded and sat. "I wouldn't have tried to drive, but I had to get back...." She shook her head and crossed her arms. I couldn't help but notice the muscles that rippled through them. I've always liked muscular arms. She wore a sleeveless flannel shirt and worn jeans. I swallowed. "I seem to be stuck."

"Yep. Lucky for you I've got a spare room. You want coffee?"

"That would be nice, thank you." She strode through a doorway and returned a few moments later with two steaming mugs. She didn't offer cream or sugar, and I didn't ask. I felt lucky that she had offered a place to sleep. "My name's Ellen James," I offered.

"They call me Marty."

I nodded and sipped at the extremely strong coffee. "I'm sorry to be a bother," I murmured. "I can pay—"

"No bother," she returned, sinking into a well-worn recliner and switching off the television. "I don't get much company. And you don't need to worry about paying."

"Well, thank you again."

She waved a large hand. Her fingers were long and unadorned. I drank my coffee and studied her surreptitiously; she had a fine figure, large firm chest and broad shoulders, no hint of extra poundage that didn't come from muscle. Her eyes were a sparkling green, her lips full and brown, and her nose long and turned up just a bit on the end.

I started to feel a little dowdy with my brown hair and eyes, my body a little rotund from all the hours spent in an office instead of outdoors. I wondered what she did for a living, but didn't dare ask. Marty took to my silence naturally, and we sat like that for at least fifteen minutes.

"Where were you headed in weather like this?" she finally asked.

"Back to town," I replied. "My boss ordered me in for some conference tomorrow."

She grinned. "You ain't gonna make it if it doesn't stop snowing."

"That's for sure."

We sat for quite a while longer, just talking, and then Marty glanced at her watch and stood up. "I'll show you to your room. You got a suitcase out in the car?"

I shook my head. "I was planning on being home before bedtime."

"So you ain't even got PJs?"

I didn't want her to know that I didn't own a pair, so I just shook my head again. She laughed and put her hand on my shoulder. The touch brought an unexpected shiver to me.

"Well, you can borrow one of my t-shirts." She showed me to a small bedroom with a single bed, a narrow dresser and a straight-back chair. There was a quilt on the bed and an afghan folded up at the foot. "Bathroom's through there," Marty said, still smiling.

"Thank you."

"I'll leave a shirt for you in here so when you come out from your shower it'll be ready. Sleep tight, Ellen James." She closed the door behind her and left me alone.

I went into the bathroom and found another door

leading out, apparently to her room, because I heard her whistling to herself. I reached down and turned on the taps for my shower, and then on impulse locked the door to her room before stripping my clothes off.

There was a t-shirt waiting, as she had promised, when I stepped out of the bathroom wrapped in a towel. I pulled it on, smelling fabric softener and the faint hint of cologne. The blankets had been turned back on the bed. With a sigh, I switched off the light and climbed in, and promptly fell asleep.

Sometime later, I came awake to a light rap at my door, followed almost instantly by the sound of the knob turning. I clutched the covers up to chin and waited.

"Ellen? You awake?" I didn't answer. Footsteps crossed the floor toward me. I felt my heart pounding, trying to imagine what she could want. "Ellen?"

"Yes?" I knew my voice was weak with fear. She pulled up short at the foot of the bed.

"You forgot to unlock my door when you finished your shower," she whispered. All my tension blew out in a long sigh. How stupid of me!

"I'm sorry."

"I just wanted you to know that's why I'm coming through here."

"What other reason could there be?" I asked lightly, though something centered in my groin was sending a message about one other possibility.

I couldn't believe I was reacting to her like that. I'd never felt attracted to another woman before. I told my sternly that it must be because my weekend with Jack had been such a disaster and tried to ignore the feeling, but it stubbornly refused to fade.

"Yeah, what other reason?" She laughed. "Well, good

night...."

When I didn't respond, she moved past my bed into the bathroom and pulled the door closed. With a sigh, I turned over and forced myself back to sleep.

The snow was still falling fiercely the next morning. I looked out the kitchen window in dismay as Marty cooked breakfast. Her coffee was as strong as before, and I drank it black.

"Well, looks like you ain't gonna make that meeting." Marty smiled.

"Looks like," I responded gloomily. "I'd better call in. My cell's in the car." I ran out and got it, and came back in just as she was setting plates on the table.

"Eat first. You can call while I do chores." We sat and ate, and then she wrapped a muffler around her neck, pulled on a checkered coat and wool gloves, and went out the back door.

I called my office and explained the situation to my boss, who wasn't happy. Then I called the cabin and spoke to Jack. He sounded almost relieved that I wasn't returning. I found myself strangely glad as well. Being stranded with Jack didn't strike me as particularly enjoyable, especially considering I had turned down his advances twice over the past two days. I didn't know what was wrong with me, because Jack was quite the catch, but he just didn't turn me on.

Marty came back in as I finished my call to him. She carried an armful of wood, which she dumped in a box next to the woodstove, throwing one piece inside the stove. After I hung up, she grinned at me. "Talking to your boyfriend?"

"He's not my boyfriend. He'd like to be, but I don't think it's going anywhere."

She laughed. I found that I liked her laugh. "Do you

play Scrabble?" I nodded. "Good. We're stuck here for the day."

We spent the rest of the day drinking coffee and playing board games. It was nice to spend time with someone like that, and I found myself remembering family vacations of my youth. We chatted about ourselves, comparing notes.

The more we talked, the more trouble I had ignoring the little ache in my groin, and I hoped she wouldn't notice the way my nipples kept getting hard when she smiled at me. I'd had fantasies about women before, strong women like Marty, but it never occurred to me I might respond to a real one, as I seemed to be responding to her.

The snow started to taper off about bed time, and I was confident that I would be able to get out the next morning. I pulled on my sleep shirt and crawled under the covers, and tried to go to sleep. Perhaps an hour passed, and then I heard Marty tapping on my door as she had the night before. Half-asleep, I wondered if I had forgotten to unlock the bathroom door again.

"Come in," I called.

She slipped through the door and came to the foot of the bed. "Did I wake you?"

"No." I waited for her to tell me what she was there for. I heard her shift from one foot to the other, and then she walked up to the side of the bed and sat down on it. "Is something wrong?"

"I hope not." She stopped me when I started to reach for the light. "Ellen…."

"Yes?"

"I…." She paused, and then muttered, "Oh, Hell."

I sensed her movement even as I felt her lips on mine, searching, hungry. I opened to her first in shock, then as her tongue delved into my mouth, with my own desire. I reached up to encircle her shoulders with my arms and felt her shudder. Her lips moved from mine to my neck.

"Marty...." How could I feel such a sudden hunger for this woman, for any woman? The question rose and faded back into insignificance quickly. I felt the hunger, and that was all I could focus on.

She pulled back the covers and lifted me into her arms, her mouth coming back to mine. I felt the hardness of her nipples through her nightshirt as she pressed me to her chest. She stood and with surprising ease maneuvered me through the bathroom and into her bedroom, and then deposited me gently on her double bed. Only then did she take her lips from my mouth.

"I've got an awful ache for you," she whispered. "I was afraid I'd read you wrong."

She'd read me better than I could have read myself. I was shocked at the hunger in my voice when I replied, "Not wrong at all."

Her hands came to my shoulders and traced down across my chest. She felt the rigid buds of my nipples with her fingers and smiled. I wanted to feel her against me and reached to draw her down. She kept smiling and evaded my hands, then gently pushed up my t-shirt to reveal my breasts.

I pulled the shirt off, and lay there in just my briefs, which were rapidly becoming soaked through. Only in my so-often-denied fantasies had I found myself so ready—so hotly needy—so fast. The look of hunger on her face sent jolts of lightning racing through me.

"You're stunning," she whispered, her hands coming back to my breasts and nipples, squeezing and releasing them.

"Take your shirt off," I pleaded. "I want to see you."

She complied, and I was rewarded with my first real look at her heavy bosom, the nipples rock hard erections against the puckering brown circles from which they rose. When I reached for her this time, she didn't resist, and I took her breasts in my hands with a sigh. They fit against my fingers as though made to rest there. I let her go long enough to slip my arms down to her waist, and pulled her to me.

Marty let out a long moan when our chests met, and I felt my insides turning to jelly. Her weight pressed me into the mattress as we lay full length on full length, our mouths moving together. Instinctively, I spread my legs and felt the sharp shock of arousal as her hips pressed between mine.

I was almost wanton in my desire to have her, to feel her. My hands moved to the waistband of her boxers, pushing them down. She lifted herself from me long enough to remove them and my briefs as well, and then pressed back down against me. Her eyes widened slightly.

"You're so wet," she groaned. "Dear God, so wet…."

"Take me," I whispered, the thought feeding my hunger.

I lifted my legs around her and pulled her to me, but she wasn't ready. She slipped down my body so that her mouth was at my breast, and she closed her lips around first one nipple then the other, suckling like a baby. I arched my back at the spears of energy that shot toward my groin, my fingernails raking at her back.

No man had ever made me feel like this. I had thought myself unworthy of them because I couldn't respond to my lovers the way they wanted me to. Now I knew why. There was nothing Marty could do to me that I wouldn't want from her, nothing that could make me want her less. All my life had been spent waiting for this one night, for the night I found this.

I was moving against her now, pressing my hips up into her belly with growing urgency, feeling the wetness flowing from me covering her. Her hand came to my thigh, moved within, and I stilled as I felt her fingers delve into the tangle of hair, between my swollen lips.

She groaned again, the vibration against my nipple even more arousing because of the long slow strokes she was making with her hand. She came to the hardened center of my need, moved across it firmly, and then slipped her fingers inside me. I thrust against her, taking her into me with a loud guttural noise.

"Oh, God," I murmured, my hands in her hair. "Take me. God, take me hard...."

She began to move inside me, her fingers pressing in as her mouth turned rough on my breasts, her teeth biting at the nipples. I was helpless under the onslaught, able only to moan my desire, beg her to make me come.

"Come for me," she whispered just as I began to think I could hold back no longer. "Ellen ... baby ... come for me."

My back arching, I did, feeling the ball of heat that had been building in my stomach explode outward like a supernova, obliterating everything but the pulsing spasms of my orgasm, feeling my muscles capture her fingers as wet warmth rushed out over them.

Finally, the feeling started to fade, but her hand was moving again, and she slipped further down my body to kneel between my legs. She buried her face against my wetness and another explosion totally engulfed me.

My hands clawed into the bedspread, my thighs clamped shut on her head as her tongue danced eagerly over the swollen wetness of my lips. She kept at me until I wanted to sob, and then stopped; her fierceness turned tender in a heartbeat. She came up beside me and gathered me into her arms, rocking me gently as I drew in wracked breaths.

"Thank you, thank you," she murmured, kissing me softly.

I tasted myself on her and wanted with a sudden hunger to return what she had done. She had my head cradled against her chest, and it was easy for me to turn my face and take one of her rigid nipples in my mouth. With a contented sigh, I began to suck on it. Marty made a strangled sound and pressed against my mouth.

I could never have imagined that it could be so satisfying to suck a woman's breasts. I kissed and licked and sucked on them until she was begging me to take her. Finally, I rolled her over onto her back and moved between her legs, my hand seeking out the raging heat of her passion. Her clitoris was swollen and erect, her inner lips soaked with her wetness. I explored her, the folds and crevices of her, then dipped my fingers inside her and felt her pulling me in.

I was struck with an unexpected and undeniable desire to taste her, so I moved down to add my lips to my fingers. There are no words to describe the delicious sweetness of her. For a long while, I let my hand be still as I simply ran my tongue over her, relishing the taste and feel of her, the way her hips jerked when I passed over her clitoris, the moans elicited when I lapped at her with long slow strokes. Her hands were woven into my hair, her head turning from side to side erratically. Finally, somehow sensing that she was close to climax, I began to move my fingers and was rewarded with an almost instantaneous rush of sticky wetness from her.

"Oh, God, Ellen … oh, yes … God, yes…."

"Come for me," I breathed. "Come on … be a good girl…."

"Yes! Yes, yes, yesyes*yesGOD!*" Then she coming, her voice raised to a scream as she cried out my name and I tasted the fullness of her under my lips. I kept thrusting with my hand until she reached and stopped me, shuddering one last time.

She drew me up beside her and kissed me. We lay together for a silent while, and then Marty rose up and moved over me. So it would go for the rest of the night.

The sun was shining when I awoke the next morning. I opened my eyes to find myself curled up next to this strong red-head who was watching me with clear green eyes. My body felt renewed, replenished. When she saw that I was awake, Marty raised her hand and brushed the hair out of my eyes.

"Good morning." Her voice was soft.

Blushing, I remembered the events of the prior night. "Morning."

"Regrets?" Her face clouded a little.

"Only that I have to leave." And it was true. I regretted nothing, save that and that it had taken me thirty years to figure out what I really wanted—a woman like Marty.

"Do you? I suppose you do. Back to the big city and your life." She stretched and climbed out of bed. I watched muscles ripple across her bare back, saw the long red scratch marks left by my nails.

"Oh! I hurt you!"

She glanced over her shoulder at her reflection in the mirror and grinned. "Love marks, darlin'. But if you're going to make a habit of sleeping with women you'd better cut those things."

"Marty…." She looked at me expectantly. "Thank you."

"My pleasure."

Over breakfast, I contemplated what I would tell Jack.

Nothing. I'd just politely return his sports car and ask him to leave my cabin. I wondered what Marty would think if I invited her up for the weekend. I put the question to her and she grinned broadly.

"I'd love to."

I reached over, took her hand, and gave it a squeeze. "I'm glad. I'll cut my nails this time."

That was almost a year ago. I wake up in the morning now and look over at her, and I wonder what it is that makes one person love another, the way that I love her. If it's fate or luck or personality, I don't know. And I don't care. We've had our share of ups and downs, but every day we grow closer and stronger. And in the end, love is all that matters.

Taking a Ride

Vicky Smythe

"God, when did Daytona Beach get so boring?" Deanna Wilcox sighed heavily and leaned forward, resting her elbows on the bar.

"It didn't." Kelly smirked. "You just got old." When Deanna growled at her, she laughed aloud. "Come on, Deanna, you can't tell me there's not someone in here you think is worth buying a drink."

Deanna toyed with the label on her beer bottle and looked around the room. It wasn't packed, but it certainly wasn't empty either. Problem was, it looked more like a high school dance than a lesbian bar, at least to her.

"And when did twenty-two year olds start looking so young?" she asked with a grimace.

Kelly shrugged. "They'll look even younger when you hit forty, let me tell you. What happened with you and Tammy?"

"She wanted to pick out matching towels and I wasn't ready to get out of the pool."

"There's half your problem right there," Kelly responded. "Women your age are starting to look at settling down; if you aren't looking at the twenty-something's, you're going to spend a lot more nights alone."

Deanna snorted. "I'm only thirty-two." *I don't feel old enough to be settling down. Hell, I don't feel old enough to be left unsupervised.* She wondered if maybe that had something to do with it; she certainly hadn't outgrown her wild twenties the way her friends had.

Kelly raised an eyebrow. "And your point is?"

"What's wrong with good old-fashioned meaningless sex?"

"There are other ways to be entertained on a Friday night besides sex." Kelly rolled her eyes. "As shocking as that may sound to you."

Deanna drained her beer. "Sure. Dozens. None nearly as much—Hello!"

The woman who had made Deanna's head snap around stood just inside the door, scanning the room with an expression that suggested she was waiting for her eyes—blue, Deanna thought, though it was hard to tell from so many feet away—to adjust to the dimness. Her dirty-blonde hair was pulled back from an oval face and fell around her shoulders with a hint of a curl. She was slightly above average height and muscular in the way that women who enjoy sports tend to be.

Deanna let out a low whistle, loud enough only for Kelly to hear. "Ye-owza!"

"She looks kind of high class, don't you think, Dee?" Kelly glanced at the woman and then looked back at Deanna with a slightly disapproving frown. "A little young for you, too. Don't go hitting on tourists before they even finish a drink."

Deanna waved dismissively. "She's a hot number. Doesn't mean I want to take her home." *Oh, but I do. Take her home and fuck the high class right out of her.* She coughed.

"And yeah, a little young." *And supple, don't forget supple.*

The woman seemed finally to decide where she was going, and where she was going was directly toward Deanna. She walked with a slow saunter, hips moving in a way that told Deanna she was wearing heels even before she got close enough for confirmation. She was indeed wearing heels; not quite stiletto heels attached to long leather boots into which her almost-too-tight jeans were tucked.

As she drew closer, Deanna confirmed that her eyes were, in fact, blue. Surprisingly, she didn't appear as young as she had from a distance; twenty-eight, perhaps, but not much younger. *Not too young after all.* Her brown lips were curled into a half-smile as she slid onto the barstool next to where Deanna sat trying to look cool.

"Is this seat taken?" Her voice was a low purr and her gaze took Deanna in with a long, apparently approving, sweep.

"It is now," Deanna returned with a grin. The night was suddenly looking infinitely more interesting.

The woman ordered a rum and coke before glancing at Deanna once again. "Have we met?"

It wasn't the most original line, but Deanna didn't care; she wasn't looking for witty repartee. "I don't think so. I'm Deanna."

"Lauren," the blonde replied, studying her more closely. "You do look familiar. Wishful thinking, maybe." She laughed.

"I'm pretty sure I'd remember meeting *you.*" Deanna grinned again. "You aren't from around here, are you?"

Lauren paid for the drink Kelly sat in front of her and took a sip before shaking her head. "No, up near Gainesville. I'm just down for a long weekend."

"By yourself?" Deanna asked casually before draining

her beer and gesturing for another one.

"Yes," Lauren replied with a quick laugh, "although my mother is certain I'm going to fall victim to some serial killer for coming alone."

Deanna laughed as well. "I'm pretty sure you're safe on that."

"She thinks I'm so sweet and naïve I'm bound to come to no good end." Lauren rolled her eyes.

"And you aren't sweet and naïve?" Deanna looked at the plunging neckline of Lauren's blouse and decided it wasn't likely.

Lauren shook her head. "Not in the least."

Quite pleased with the response, Deanna indicated the half-empty glass in the woman's hand. "Let me buy you the next one."

"I won't turn down a free drink," Lauren replied, once again smiling. "After all, this is my weekend to cut loose."

"Cutting loose once in a while is always a good thing." Deanna waved at Kelly and indicated their drinks. "Even if it does mean risking death by serial killer."

They both laughed, and then fell into a comfortable conversation. Deanna found that despite her initial assumption, Lauren was quite witty and well-read, and generally fascinating in a way she hadn't been fascinated in a very long time. An hour passed, and then Deanna became aware that Lauren was flirting with her. It was very subtle, but the subtlety made it even more interesting.

"So, what are your plans for the weekend, other than helping me hold up the bar?" she finally inquired, looking for an opening to suggest something less vertical.

Lauren's smile was slow and seductive. "I hadn't really thought past tonight, but I was hoping you'd be interested in a less public joint venture." Her gaze was even but her eyes held a promise that Deanna wouldn't be left disappointed.

Deanna blinked twice. "I was thinking the same thing," she said a moment later, both excited by the prospect and a little startled at Lauren's unexpected bluntness.

"Good." The blonde shifted, her hand sliding easily onto Deanna's thigh. "I'm not usually this forward, but I didn't want to let you get away."

"Did you have something specific in mind?" Deanna grinned. She had plenty of ideas if Lauren came up empty-handed.

Lauren's hand moved a little further up and in. "How far away is the beach?"

"About ten minutes. Five if we take my bike."

"You ride?" Lauren's smile spread. "Even better."

Deanna put her hand atop Lauren's and ran her fingers up the woman's arm. "I love to ride."

"Then what are we waiting for?"

Ignoring Kelly's disapproving look, Deanna knocked back the last of her beer and stood up, offering Lauren her hand. Lauren took it, and they went out to the parking lot, stopping beside Deanna's Harley.

"You want my helmet?" Deanna asked.

Lauren stepped closer and leaned in to kiss her; it was a soft, teasing kiss that set off an ache between Deanna's legs. "I like to live dangerously," the blonde replied in a seductive whisper.

"Dangerously it is." Deanna threw her leg over the seat, fit the key into the lock and hit the ignition; the bike roared to life. "Hop on and hold tight."

Once Lauren was snugged up behind her, arms wrapped low around Deanna's waist, Deanna aimed the motorcycle north toward the more deserted end of the beach and accelerated.

Taking a Ride

It took a little more than five minutes, but soon enough they were parked by a set of access stairs looking out over the ocean. The moon had started to rise, shimmering off the water and illuminating the sand just enough to make out the tiny wavelets running up on shore.

"You ever had sex on the beach?" Deanna glanced at her companion, thinking she probably hadn't, if the look on her face was any indication. She was clearly not concerned about the likelihood of sand ending up in places she might find less than enjoyable.

Lauren looked back at her, eyes almost glowing in the pale moonlight. "No. You seem hesitant though; something I should know?"

"It may not be as romantic as you're thinking," Deanna replied. "Just warning you."

"Romance isn't on my mind at the moment. But I think I catch your meaning." Lauren looked back over the waves. "Damn."

Deanna considered her for a moment. "There's always the stairs. Just fine for what I want to do."

Lauren grinned. "Close enough."

They reached the bottom steps before turning to one another. Deanna's heart started to pound in anticipation of what was to come; Lauren was long and lean and obviously as ready as she was. When she reached up to touch Lauren's face, the woman smiled seductively.

"Is there anything you don't want me to do?" Deanna knew that once she had Lauren's jeans off, she wasn't going to want to fumble around. She dropped her hand to the blonde's shoulder, tracing the side of her neck with one finger.

"Don't rip my blouse." Lauren brought her hands to Deanna's waist. "Other than that, the book is wide open."

They stopped talking then, letting their mouths continue the conversation in much closer quarters and without words. Lauren's lips were soft, her tongue readily meeting Deanna's in a velvet dance as their hands began exploring one another more intimately. *She's a damn good kisser.* Deanna thought that boded well for what was to come.

She slid her hands between their bodies and started unbuttoning Lauren's blouse, biting her way down the woman's long neck to her shoulder, her tongue tracing the line of collarbone as it was revealed when she pulled the fabric open. Lauren shuddered. Deanna finished undoing the buttons and slid the blouse down her arms, carefully folding it in half and laying it over the railing before coming back to remove her bra.

Lauren's breasts were firm, not quite large enough to hang against her ribcage, her nipples surprisingly thick and dark. Deanna drank them in with her eyes before reaching up to run light fingers across the upper curve of each breast and then down to trace the outline of the puckered circles from which those now hardened buds rose. Lauren shuddered again and arched her back slightly.

Licking her lips, Deanna closed her fingers on Lauren's nipples and squeezed lightly. Lauren groaned and she squeezed a little harder, rolling her fingers and pulling at the tips.

"Oh, God...." Lauren drew in a deep breath. "Harder."

Deanna complied and felt another, stronger shudder pass through the woman's body. She bent her head and pressed her lips against Lauren's as she twisted her fingers, pulling away and letting go with a sharp snapping motion. She ran a lazy, hot line down Lauren's neck, to her chest, and down around one rigid bud, nipping at it before drawing it into her mouth as her hand reclaimed its twin.

Lauren's breath grew ragged and she lifted a hand to the back of Deanna's head, holding her against her breast. Deanna closed her lips and flicked rapidly at the tip of the nipple in her mouth, feeling Lauren's response with a hungry pleasure. She drew back and let the nipple scrape through her teeth before kissing to the second to repeat her attentions. Finally, when she sensed Lauren's legs trembling, she lifted her hands and undid the woman's belt and the button of her jeans.

The boots proved slightly problematic, but Deanna managed to get them off and finished stripping Lauren's clothes from her body. She was as careful with these as she had been the blouse, and came back between Lauren's legs as she knelt on a lower step.

"You like it as rough on your clit?" she asked, sliding her hands up the insides of Lauren's thighs. She could just see the silvery wetness in the surprisingly light blonde hair that covered Lauren's center, and smiled to herself. *She's certainly ready to go.*

"Yes," Lauren replied, spreading her legs farther apart. "You've got me aching for your mouth."

Deanna grinned and bent forward, taking little bites along one of Lauren's inner thighs as she worked her way closer to her goal, her fingers brushing against the tangle of hair ever-so-lightly. When she reached the join of the blonde's hip, she pressed in with her hands and spread Lauren's lips; with a hungry growl she claimed the swollen heat within with her mouth, her tongue eagerly seeking Lauren's hardened tip.

Lauren groaned and lifted her hands to Deanna's head. Deanna danced against her clit before dropping her face and slipping her tongue into the source of the wetness that coated her chin and lips. She lapped upward, again catching the rigid bud at the top of Lauren's mons, this time sucking it into her mouth and biting against it lightly with her teeth.

"Yes...." The word was a hiss as Lauren lifted against Deanna's mouth. Deanna lashed at her clit with her tongue, feeling her writhe as her teeth tightened at the base. "God, yes, like ... that—"

Deanna smiled to herself and let the nub slide from her lips, returning to make another series of slow, languid laps from bottom to top, teasingly flicking at Lauren's clit before dropping down again. Lauren started squirming, and Deanna lifted a hand to press two fingers against the woman's well.

"How many do you want?" she pressed slightly deeper.

"Two ... three ... I don't care—just fuck me, please!" Lauren's voice was pleading, breathy. She let out a short scream as Deanna thrust into her with three fingers, and then moaned when, a moment later, Deanna caught her clitoris between her teeth once again and started sucking on it.

Deanna could tell it wouldn't take long to bring her to climax, and wasted no more time with teasing. She thrust hard with her fingers, feeling the shivers of pleasure rippling through Lauren's legs, lashed at her clit with her tongue and bit at it with her teeth. Lauren was groaning and lifting against her and then, suddenly, her fingers tangled into Deanna's hair and she arched her back, exploding into orgasm with a, "yesyes—ohgod—*ohyes*—GOD—*YES*!" that was almost loud enough to be worrisome, given their location.

After several long seconds of spasms, she finally let go of Deanna's head and went limp. Deanna withdrew her fingers, ran her tongue once more across Lauren's clit—rewarded with a final shudder and gasped, "enough!"—and sat back on her knees.

"God. Damn. Deanna!" After a long indrawn breath, Lauren sat up and looked at her, her face flushed. "You take direction well."

Deanna smiled. "Thank you." She studied the woman before her for a moment. "Caught your breath?"

Lauren's eyes seemed to glow. "Yes." She reached out and pulled at Deanna's t-shirt. "Your turn."

Deanna stripped quickly, taking much less care with her own clothes than she had with Lauren's, and crawled up to offer her breasts to Lauren's mouth. Lauren was eager, drawing in a nipple and sucking at it while her fingers sought its sister. Deanna allowed her time to enjoy tasting and teasing before moving further up and kneeling again with Lauren's head between her thighs.

"Be careful," she said with a grin. "You've got me so wet you may have trouble breathing."

Lauren laughed and took her by the hips. "I can hold my breath a long time," she replied before pulling Deanna down against her mouth, her tongue burrowing into Deanna's wet hair, exploring her and finally capturing her clit.

"Oh, God...." Deanna groaned and grabbed at the rails, relishing the jolts of pleasure that coursed through her with each flick of Lauren's tongue. *Damn, she's good at this!* "That feels so...."

Lauren made a noise that might have been a giggle, and tightened her hands on Deanna's hips, hardening her tongue and sliding it into the source of Deanna's wetness with a deft thrust. Deanna shuddered and pressed her hips forward. Lauren filled her again and then resumed a languid lapping motion that drew short gasps from Deanna and made her legs start shivering.

After a few minutes, Lauren shifted and brought up her hand, pressing two fingers into Deanna's center as her tongue moved up and began to dart against her clit once more. Deanna groaned more loudly and started moving against her.

"Yes ... Lauren ... just ... oh, God!" The sensation of the blonde's fingers filling her, coupled with the liquid heat of her tongue, sent waves of pleasure washing over Deanna's body.

Within a very few minutes it was Deanna who was gasping and begging and trying to swallow the scream that climax threatened to rip from her throat. After a final spasm, Deanna pulled back and half-collapsed on the steps beside Lauren, trying to catch her breath. Lauren was watching her with a grin that suggested she had enjoyed herself immensely.

"You were right, you were wet," the blonde said after a moment, wiping her face across her arm. "Did you get enough?"

Deanna managed to nod. "I'd love another round, but we shouldn't sit here naked too long. It is a public access."

Lauren hesitated, and Deanna got the impression she was debating how to respond. Finally, she laughed and looked up at the moon. "That's a bail money call I'd rather not make."

"Your clothes shouldn't be too wrinkled." Deanna reached for them.

"Thank you." Lauren started getting dressed. "I noticed you took care with them."

Deanna shrugged and snagged her jeans. "A beautiful woman should look as beautiful after sex as before."

Lauren paused in buttoning her blouse and looked at her, her face coloring slightly. "I don't get called that too often."

"Then you're hanging around the wrong people." Deanna coughed and turned to find her t-shirt.

"Maybe I am." Lauren laughed again. "The sex is definitely better here than at home."

"You're not too bad yourself."

They grinned at each other and finished getting dressed, and then Deanna took Lauren back to the bar. Standing in the parking lot by Lauren's sedan, they studied one another silently.

"Do you come here often?" Lauren finally asked, gesturing toward the building.

Deanna shrugged, wanting to sound casual. "Depends."

"Do you think you'll be here tomorrow night?" Lauren's eyes offered a repeat performance should the answer be yes.

"I don't see why not."

Lauren smiled slowly. "Hopefully we'll meet again, then."

"I hope so, too," Deanna replied. "I'm up for another ride."

"More than one maybe?"

"I'm up for that too." Deanna smiled softly. "Somewhere less public."

Lauren kissed her on the cheek and winked. "Much less public."

Deanna watched her leave and then turned and strolled back into the bar. A couple more drinks and she'd head home and catch some shut-eye. It had turned out to be a very entertaining Friday night after all.

LIGHTNING

Rebecca Montague

Sometimes, I wonder what would have happened if Sophie hadn't dumped me when she did. Almost six weeks we were together, and never a complaint. The sex was good, and I thought we had plenty in common. I guess Sophie didn't see it that way. I'm still not sure exactly what happened, but then, I never was exactly sure why women left me.

So, anyway, I'd nursed the hurt for a week of interminable days, and now it was Friday and I didn't have to look at another thirteen year old for 64 consecutive hours. Don't get me wrong, my job's fine. There are worse things you can do than teach middle school PE. But at the end of the week, I'm ready for some adult entertainment and someone who doesn't call me 'Coach Arnett'.

That Friday, instead of heading to my favorite hangout, I was driving forty minutes out of town to visit Cori Witherspoon. She wasn't my absolute best friend, but she was close, the one who always seemed to make it better when I had worries. I'd known Cori for nearly five years by then. She'd suffered through numerous breakups with me, always smiling and telling me in that gruff voice of hers that the sooner I stopped looking for love, the sooner love would find me. I guess I'm thick-headed, because I never did listen.

To me, love was supposed to come out of the blue and strike you right between the ribs the first time you kissed someone. Problem was, it never quite worked out that way, and lately I'd started to think that maybe I was getting hit a little too low. About eighteen inches too low, if you catch my meaning.

Anyway, Cori is a couple of years older than me, and the most divine interpretation of a butch ever to walk this earth. She's nearly six feet tall, muscular in a way that takes women hours at the gym to achieve. She keeps her blonde hair cut high and tight. She has the sort of face that stops conversations whenever she enters the room, helped by blue eyes that could melt through steel. I'd overheard more than one early twenty-something baby dyke in town say that they didn't care if she was almost thirty-five; they wouldn't turn her down if she offered to drive them home in that big black Ford pickup of hers.

Thing is, Cori never offered. Some women thought she was conceited, but for most of them, it just made her even more mysterious and exciting. I couldn't recall the last relationship she'd been in, but she didn't seem to mind much. She lived on a farm outside of town, so I guessed she liked her solitude.

I always felt slightly awed next to Cori. I don't think I'm unattractive, maybe a seven out of ten as far as dykes go, but to me Cori is a knockout of mythical proportions. She was easy to be friends with, though. She knew me way too well to ever consider dating me, which was fine with me because I'd have hated to lose her friendship over something as meaningless as sex.

We had a lot in common as far as interests go; wine, food, horses and music. I spent the weekend out at her place every couple of months, and we would fix elaborate gourmet meals, drink wine, and strum our guitars until the wee hours of the morning. We even slept in the same bed sometimes, curled together like old lovers.

That Friday I was just driving up for the evening, to vent and get a couple of Cori's magical healing hugs. The weatherman was announcing doom and gloom for the weekend, but I didn't pay it much mind. Thunderstorms aren't exactly unusual in the spring down here in South Carolina. The drive out to the farm was peaceful, down a couple of two lane highways that led from Greenville back up into the hills. The farm is just outside of Tigerville, a town small enough its population isn't even listed in the back of the road atlas. A light rain had started to fall as I turned off the paved road onto the dirt one that led to Cori's. I drove over Cane Creek on the bridge Cori and her brother had built out of railroad ties a few years earlier after it washed away in a flood, and considered myself officially in the sticks once I'd made it successfully across.

It was maybe a quarter mile further to Cori's house. The rain was increasing by the time I pulled up next to her truck in the front yard of the house, so I made a dash for it and called her name as I stepped through the door. I never knocked at Cori's house. She would have been insulted if I had. But that's just Cori. She came out of the kitchen with a glass of wine in her hand and one of her patented grins on her face. I took the wine and hugged and kissed her hello. I always counted myself lucky that I got to kiss her like that; not too many women I knew of did.

"I wasn't sure you were coming, Beverly," Cori commented. "Radar looks pretty nasty."

"What, and miss the pleasure of your company?" I grinned back at her.

Cori snorted. "More likely my wine," she retorted good-naturedly, and winked. "Come on into the den and tell me your woes."

Feeling much better already, I followed her through the house.

* * *

The first distant roll of thunder reached us as we sat down in the den. I could hear the raindrops dancing off the metal roof. It was a calming sound. Cori took her usual seat in an old leather recliner and I sat on the end of the couch next to her.

"How's life treating you?" I sipped my wine and waited to hear what new project she had launched since we last talked. She built furniture, and did it well.

"Fine. I got a commission to build a sleigh bed, so I'm enjoying that. I went with oak." Cori ran her fingers along the arm of the chair. "You sounded pretty upset on Monday. How are you doing?"

I shrugged. "I don't know. I really thought it was going to work out this time."

Cori studied me. "Did she give you a reason?"

"Not really. She said she didn't think we were a good fit. I sure thought we were. And I just bought new water skis because I thought we were going to take the boat over to Lake Keowee so she could teach me."

"You hate water skiing." Cori rolled her eyes. "I thought the whole concept terrified you."

"Well, it does ... kind of ... but Sophie was really into it," I answered guiltily. I really didn't like the idea behind water skiing, but I always made an effort to fit in with my lovers' interests. From the way Cori was looking at me, I guessed she thought that wasn't a good thing.

"That's half your problem," she said firmly. "You lose yourself in your girlfriend. How can someone love you if they don't know who you are?"

"I'm starting to see that. But what if just being me isn't interesting enough?"

"You're plenty interesting." Cori laughed. "You're just trying too hard. You and Sophie were all wrong for each other."

"Why didn't you say something when we first started dating?" The sound of the rain on the roof was intensifying, and the thunder sounded much closer.

Cori shrugged. "I learned a long time ago to stay out of your way when you take an interest in someone. There's nothing worse than a nosy friend telling you the romance of your dreams is going to turn into a nightmare."

As much as I hated to admit it, I had to agree with her. When I took a shining to a woman, I did tend to become a little single minded in my pursuit. I would have gotten irritated if she'd tried to warn me off about Sophie in the beginning. "You're right." I sighed. "Yet again. I hate that."

"I'm not always right," Cori returned wryly. "If I were, I'd be happily partnered by now. It's just easier to point out someone else's mistakes."

"If you ever found Miss Right you'd break half the hearts in Greenville." I laughed and finished my wine.

"Please. Like I need a bunch of horny twenty-two year olds following me around like puppy dogs. I'm more into the sensitive, romantic type." Cori twisted her mouth into a quirky grin. "Someone who actually remembers when cars came with tape players."

"Oh, an old fart like yourself, then?" I laughed when she swatted my hand. "Well, you'll never find Miss Right hiding out here all the time. You need to come into town more often."

"We aren't talking about me, we're talking about you," Cori reminded me sternly. "Let me get more wine and we'll do just that."

We talked for a couple of hours, reaching the same conclusions as we always did, that I was so busy looking for love it would probably bite me before I realized it was standing there. Cori, in her usual comforting way, had talked me through the hurt of Sophie's leaving until I admitted that the hurt boiled down into disappointment with myself for making yet another wrong choice. Next time, I vowed, I'd wait until I knew for certain I was right before I gave my heart away again. Cori was supportive, though probably not convinced because I'd made the same vow before.

The storm had risen to a raging fury by the time we finished the bottle of wine and I was ready to leave. I opened the front door and looked outside. The dirt road leading past Cori's house bore a frightening resemblance to a muddy river. Water pooled around my car and stood in large puddles around the yard. Cori looked past my shoulder at the road and whistled.

"Shit. That doesn't bode well. You'd better let me check the bridge before you take off."

"My hero," I replied with a grin. "I suppose you think your monster truck won't get stuck as quickly as my sedan?"

She stuck her tongue out. "Now you're just being idiotic. I'm the butch; let me do my job."

"Aye, aye, Captain." I threw a mock salute at her. "Let

me know if the passage is clear."

She grabbed her keys off the table by the door and dashed out into the rain. I watched the water spray as she backed out of the driveway and into the stream that was supposed to be a road. She drove off toward the bridge slowly, and returned—long enough later that I was getting worried—with her truck covered in mud. She climbed down from the cab and ran back to the house.

"Creek's flooding," she said as lightning flashed overhead, followed immediately by a loud clap of thunder. Small hail began to pelt down. Cori closed the door behind her and ran a hand through her hair. Water dripped off her sweatshirt. "Bobby and I bolted that bridge down good, but from the looks of it, it could go any time now. I'd really rather not tempt fate."

"Ah, stranded in the clutches of Greenville's most eligible bachelorette. Oh, fate worse than death." Cori made a face and punched me playfully in the arm. "Hey! That hurt."

"Bullshit. How do you feel about spaghetti Bolognese and a bottle of Chianti? There must be something worth watching on TV tonight."

"Sounds great. I'll chop, you stir."

We retired to the kitchen to make dinner. I had managed to prep most of the vegetables when the lights flickered. Outside, a brilliant flash of lightning exploded, followed instantly by a thunderclap loud enough to make me start to duck. The lights went out completely, and stayed out. After a couple of seconds, I felt Cori slip by me and heard her fumbling through a drawer. She turned on a flashlight and pulled open the kitchen door to look into the backyard.

"Well, shit. Transformer's blown." She closed the door

and faced me. "I guess TV's out."

"What about your generator?" I knew she had a backup generator for winter outages.

She sighed. "I haven't got any gas. That was on my list for this weekend. Hang on; I'll go get some lamps."

She disappeared in the direction of the spare bedroom and returned with a cardboard box. She pulled four oil lamps out, selected one, lit a match and held it to the mantle. When it caught, she lowered the chimney and adjusted the flame. I noticed in the soft glow that the stove was still on. I'd forgotten she didn't have an electric pilot on her range.

"At least we can still eat," I commented. "I'm sure we can find something to amuse ourselves with later."

"I'm sure." Without another word, she pulled a bottle of wine out of the rack and reached for the corkscrew.

* * *

After eating dinner by lamp light, we opened yet another bottle of wine and retired to the den. Cori started a fire in her woodstove and we sat together on the couch as we often did, with me leaning against her and her arm draped across the back of the couch behind me. I liked sitting like that with her. It was very comfortable. We were illuminated by the glow of two oil lamps. The conversation turned to romance.

"So, who is your ideal mate?"

Cori looked at me strangely. "I don't know, someone intelligent, romantic, not too femme though. I hate the taste of lipstick."

"Me too. I'm more the butch type myself. As long as there are brains under the muscle." I glanced toward the fireplace.

"Really? You haven't dated many butch women that I remember." Cori ran her finger around the rim of her glass thoughtfully.

I shrugged. "There aren't too many around who fit my requirements and aren't taken."

"What other requirements do you have?"

"Well ... intelligence, a sense of humor, she'd have to like the outdoors, good wine, good food. Fishing. She'd definitely have to like fishing. Independent enough not to need me every second of every day but romantic enough to let me pamper her. Uhmmm ... good in bed; that's always a bonus. Like I said, there aren't too many women out there who measure up to all that."

Cori was silent for a minute. "What about me?"

I stared at her for a second before laughing. "Right. Like I'm anything close to your type. Nice one, Cori."

"I didn't say anything about my type," she responded quietly. "I asked if I fit your 'requirements'."

I considered her question for a moment. "Yes, I suppose you do," I replied finally. "But you're my friend. I'd have known a long time ago if you were the least bit interested. I'm sure I'm too plain for your tastes anyway."

She shifted and brought her arm down onto my shoulders so naturally I didn't really register her movement at first. "I happen to think you're beautiful." Her voice was a soft purring growl.

I looked at her. She was studying me with those blue eyes of hers, the ones that could melt through steel. Only what they were melting through was me. I saw a deep want in her eyes, a want I had never seen there before. Her gaze was steady, bright.

I leaned forward and put my wine glass down on the coffee table. She didn't make an effort to move when I turned so that I was facing her. "Are you drunk?" Her expression had awakened an ache in me, and there was no way I was going to let this go on if she wasn't sober. I wasn't about to let wine or a romantic situation or anything else ruin our friendship.

Slowly, she smiled. It was a brilliant smile that lit her face until she practically glowed. "No, I'm not. But thank you for considering it. Am I scaring you?"

I shook my head. "No. But … you do … seem to be coming on to me."

Her laugh sent a chill of desire down my spine. "You're very observant, Beverly."

"But you don't … I mean … all the nights we've slept together … you've never—"

She cut me off with a kiss that made me glad I had put my glass down, because I would have certainly spilled my wine. Her mouth was soft, passionate, and hungry. Her tongue danced with the most delicate of touches against mine. I'm usually the one making the first move, and the gently questioning way with which her hands reached to pull me closer made my heart skip a beat. She enfolded me in an embrace unlike any she had ever held me in.

"I have now," she whispered as she moved her lips to my ear. I felt a rush of desire pound through my veins, felt the fever of passion setting my skin ablaze. Her movements were studied, strong, as she sat back, reached up and traced her fingers down my cheek and across my lips. "I've wanted to for a long time."

"Why now?" My voice was weak. I wanted so very much to surrender to her, but fear tempered my desire. Fear that I was getting ready to make a big mistake.

"Was I wrong?" Her face clouded for a moment.

"No." It was the only answer I could give, and I knew as

I said it that after the next heartbeat, there would be no turning back.

Cori kissed me again, hotly, her hands moving over my back as she held me against her. I responded with a passion for her that I dimly recognized as having existed for many years. Thought fled, leaving only action. I felt her chest pressed to mine, felt the raggedness of her breathing as we parted for air.

Her fingers were sure on the buttons of my shirt, her mouth seeking mine as she slid the fabric down my shoulders. When it fell to the floor, she reached for my bra. Impatience crept into her movements as she pulled it off and tossed it over her shoulder. She leaned back and took me in with her eyes, her face betraying the depth of her hunger.

"I've imagined them so many nights," she murmured as she pushed me back across the sofa. She came on top of me, her weight pressing against me, her hands claiming my breasts. She felt the hardness of my nipples and groaned my name.

Her fingers teased me, pulling, rolling, pinching ever so lightly, and then harder, until I drew in a sharp breath of near pain. She was instantly gentle again, caressing ever so lightly. The lightness of her touch was almost harder to withstand. Just when I thought I was going to have to stop her, she pulled her hands away and dropped her head against me, her mouth closing around a hardened tip. With a deep, guttural noise, she began to suckle.

I closed my eyes and gave myself to the pleasure of her lips against my breasts, her obvious hunger feeding my own rising need. My hands moved through her hair, holding her head. Finally, she moved up my body and kissed me, and then stood. She looked down at me for a long moment before extending her hand. I sat up and took it, and allowed her to pull me to my feet. She took me in her arms, her hands cupping the curve of my backside firmly as her lips moved over my face and down my neck. She buried her face against the crook of my neck and shoulder and bit against the muscle. Lightning exploded in the vicinity of my belly.

I moved to pull her sweatshirt off. Underneath, she wore only a tight scoop-necked t-shirt. Her chest was full, heaving in time with her breathing. I slid the shirt up over her head and dropped it onto the couch. Her breasts were full and firm, slightly pendulous against the curve of her ribs. The nipples rose heavily from pink circles. I took a breast in each hand, feeling the softness of the skin and the weight of them. Moving my hands slightly, I caught her tips between my fingers, tugging gently. Cori's eyes closed and she moaned.

"You're so beautiful," I whispered as I bent my head to suckle at her breast. She lifted her hand to the back of my head and crushed my face against her chest. I tasted her sweat and the sweetness of her skin against my tongue as I lapped across the hardness held gently between my teeth. Cori moaned again, more loudly.

She pulled me away and took my hand again. "Come to bed with me," she said in an almost pleading tone. I nodded and allowed her to lead me down the hall to her bedroom. Inside, we finished undressing each other hastily and fell together across the double bed, seeking each other's lips in blind passion.

Cori rolled on top of me, her hips pressing between my thighs with gentle insistence. I spread my legs and welcomed her, sliding my arms around her body as she bit down my neck to my shoulder once again, capturing me with her teeth. Her hips nudged against mine, beckoning, promising. Her hand slid between our bodies, searching out my heat. She made a soft sound as she covered her fingers in my wetness, exploring me with a gentle touch.

"God. Yes." My hips thrust upward against her hand as her fingers began to move with more purpose. She lifted away from me far enough to gaze into my face, her hand dancing against me with rapid, sure strokes. My nails bit into her back, her fingers zeroed in on the center of my passion, and I clung to her as I felt the surging tide of climax spill over me.

"Yes. Yes," she whispered as my hips jerked upwards once, twice, and then I was being washed away by a flood of pleasure that sent stars dancing behind my closed eyelids. I felt her lips on mine, felt her swallowing the cry that tore from my throat, and then all sensation whirled into a single pulsating joy that ebbed into spent exhaustion.

Cori took me in her arms and held me until the last tremors had run from my body. She kissed me gently, familiarly. I kissed her back, drawing energy from her mouth as I rolled her onto her back and came on top of her.

I caught a nipple in my mouth and held it while my fingers slid into the soft white-blonde hair between her thighs. Her wetness was obvious, her hunger swollen and ready. I explored the valleys and folds of her, discovered her with my hand, filled her with my fingers and drew the orgasm from her with a joy I had rarely known. As she clutched at the comforter and arched her back, I lifted my gaze to her face, drinking in the raw passion reflected in her eyes. It was water to my thirsty soul, her pleasure filling me and taking me to a place I was unfamiliar with yet recognized as vital to me as breathing.

We rested after that, not really speaking, me curled against her side as her hand caressed my hip. I dozed for a few minutes, awakened by her lips asking me for more. I rose and opened to her again, drew her fingers into the fount of my wetness and clung to her as she drove me to the edge once more, recognizing her need for me as merely the other side of my need for her. When the sensations overtook me, I screamed out her name, vocalizing that need the only way I could.

Into the early hours of the morning we strummed, not our guitars as we had so often in the past, but the strings of each other's desire, exploring our mutual need with our bodies. At some point, as the thunderstorm faded into the distance, we fell asleep nestled together under the tangled mess of the sheets.

* * *

Morning dawned with the bright clearness that so often follows a storm, and I woke unwillingly. Beside me, Cori had buried her face under a pillow and was snoring lightly. The clock across the room was still dark, so I slipped out of bed and padded quietly down the hall to the bathroom before fixing a quick breakfast on the stove. I counted myself lucky as I poured coffee from the percolator that I was familiar enough with one not to create sludge, then pulled a tray off the refrigerator and returned to the bedroom with the food.

Cori shifted as I climbed back onto the bed, and pulled the pillow away from her face. She squinted over at me, and then smiled. "Good morning," she said softly.

"Morning, beautiful." I slid the tray forward. "I fixed a bite to eat."

Cori stretched and gazed at me evenly. "You're an angel, you know that?"

I smiled and waved dismissively. "I'm pretty sure the coffee won't curl your toes." I handed her a mug.

"You did a good job of that last night." Cori sipped at the coffee and studied me over the rim. I got the impression she was waiting for some sort of sign as to how I was taking the previous night.

"With what energy you left me." I smiled and handed her a plate and then crawled next to her and picked up my own breakfast. A serious discussion of what had happened would go much more smoothly after food. And for some reason I wanted to postpone the inevitable as long as possible.

As long as possible was five minutes after we finished eating. Cori came back from the bathroom in a pair of flannel boxer shorts and sat down on the bed. She reached over and picked up the tray and set it on a nearby chair, then turned and took my hand.

"We need to talk about this," she said quietly. I bit my lip and nodded, not trusting my voice. "I—I'm not sure what got into me last night. I don't want it to ruin our friendship."

"Why would it?" I forced a light tone. "It was very romantic."

"Beverly, you are a very special woman. I don't think you even realize how much you have to offer. You're so … you're so damned intent on finding the woman who makes lightning strike that you aren't letting anyone get to know you."

I looked at her, unsure of what she was trying to say. "You know me better than anyone."

"We've been friends for a long time. Too long to be the one to make lightning strike, I guess." Cori looked down at our hands. "And for that I'm sorry. But I'm not sorry about how I feel."

"I never thought about lightning where you were concerned," I replied slowly. "I just liked being around you. I always figured you knew me too well to be interested in me romantically."

Cori's face took on a pained look for a moment. "I'm not very good at approaching women I like."

"I just assumed...." I trailed off and looked out the window. "I do love you."

"As a friend, yes. And I can accept that. But if we're going to be just friends then last night can't ever happen again." Cori traced her fingers along the back of my hand. "I can't share something like that without becoming emotionally involved."

I thought about the years I had known Cori, all the things we had done, all the fun we had whenever we were together. I thought about how well I knew the layout of her house, how comfortable I was walking through her front door without knocking, how easy it was to talk to her about my deepest fears. I did love her. But I loved other friends too, and the thought of kissing them was as arousing as the thought of kissing my sister. The thought of the previous night made me tremble with desire.

In all the years I had been searching for the bolt of lightning to hit me between the ribs, I never expected it to hit without any warning whatsoever. And when it did hit, it exploded in my heart with a force that shocked every fiber of my being. Cori wasn't just everything I wanted in a woman; she was the woman I had based my want on. It was no wonder I hadn't ever found The One. She was sitting next to me on the bed.

"I don't want us to just be friends," I said quietly, raising my eyes to meet her gaze. "I don't think I've ever really wanted just that."

Cori raised her eyebrows and looked at me in disbelief. Her hand tightened on mine. "Don't tease me." Her voice was low, trembling. "All these years I've hoped you would look at me as a woman, not just your friend. But I don't want you to say something you don't mean."

I raised her hand to my lips and kissed her knuckles one by one. "You are the woman I've been searching for, Cori. It took last night to show me how blind I've been. I could never do something to hurt you. I love you."

She came into my arms willingly then. I held her tightly, whispering the words I had waited years to speak, feeling the sense of oneness between our bodies. When at last the kisses turned passionate, I knew that for the first time in my life I was going to make love to a woman. There was a difference in our joining that was at once gentle and fiery. I gave myself fully to her, body and soul and heart and mind, and accepted that gift from her.

Even the most skillful lover couldn't match the satisfaction of that morning, or of any day since then. Every touch is a gift, every kiss a song, every night a poem. There is nothing about Cori that I don't love totally and completely. Lightning strikes me every time I see her smile.

FINDING ARIZONA

Vicky Smythe

I.

"Pretty slow tonight," Terri McKenzie commented as she stirred her drink with the straw.

Mick Guthrie leaned against the bar and studied the room. "Yeah, I guess. Things should pick up once the semester starts."

"God, don't remind me." Terri rolled her eyes. "To think I agreed to teach four classes this year."

"You've no one but yourself to blame," Mick returned. "You're the one that wanted to have an excuse not to spend time with Diane." When Terri shot her a pained but dirty glare, she blushed. "Sorry. But it's true."

Terri sighed. "I know. But now it means a lot of writing time wasted grading papers."

"So how's that coming?"

"Painfully slow." Terri finished her drink. "I'm beginning to wonder if it will ever be finished."

Mick shrugged. "I've heard you say that about every book you've written in the last ten years."

"The fact that you can say that is really depressing. Ten years and I've published nothing." Terri sighed again. "Fifteen, really."

"Well, I still like what you write." Mick glanced to her left and straightened up. "Looks like I have to do some actual work. Would you like another?"

"Sure."

Terri stared at the bar as Mick walked away. She played with her coaster. She brushed imaginary cigarette ash off her leg. She looked at the poster of the strongly muscled woman hanging on the wall next to her. She tried not to feel like a failure. She considered taking up smoking again. She wished school would start and distract her from the misery that had been her summer.

She and Diane had sworn they would be together always, and the run lasted twenty years. But it was over now, in the simple words that Diane had spoken over a typical dinner in late spring.

"I've found someone else." Terri had stared at her, not quite understanding what she meant until Diane spoke again. "I'm moving out. I know you can afford to buy my half of the house."

What upset Terri most was that there had been no scene, no screaming, no tears, just a stunned acceptance that two decades of love had ended. Diane left the next day, returning only to direct the movers in what to pack, and Terri hadn't begged her to stay. About a week later, what had happened really hit her and she cried, but not as long as she would've expected to. Deep inside was a part of her that was glad.

Terri frowned and finished her drink. Diane was gone, but her memory was making her miserable. She knew she had to move past it, but she wasn't sure she could. She wasn't sure she knew how to make a fresh start. She felt old and worn out.

After a while, Mick returned with a fresh drink and a strange expression. She sat the drink down and looked carefully at Terri. "The young lady at the end of the bar would like to buy this for you."

Startled, Terri looked in the direction that Mick was pointing. When Mick said young, she meant young. The woman looked to be 23 or 24, with blond hair cut high and tight in the style that baby butches favored.

"Her?" Terri stared and the woman gave her a winning smile. "She doesn't look like one of my students."

"I asked her. She doesn't know you." Mick grinned.

"Why would she want to buy me a drink?"

Mick made a face and snorted. "I have no idea. You're so damned old I can't imagine anyone buying you a drink. I mean my God, you're 50."

"So are you," Terri retorted. "Tell her thank you." She inclined her head in the woman's direction and was certain the woman winked at her.

Mick threw up her hands. "I surrender. She's probably taking one of your classes this fall and is trying to bribe you."

"Well obviously it isn't because she's interested in me. Maybe I remind her of her mother." Terri laughed. "But why turn down a free drink?"

"You're incorrigible. Would you like to send one back?"

Terri studied her. "Sure, why not? With my thanks."

Shaking her head, Mick walked off. Terri turned to her drink, glancing in the woman's direction (*Why* did *she buy me a drink?)* every once in a while. The first time that their eyes met, the woman lifted her glass and grinned and after that always seem to be looking at her when Terri glanced her way. She had almost finished her drink when the woman stood up, ran a hand through her hair and walked toward her.

"Hi," she said as she came up. "A good looking woman like you shouldn't be sitting alone. Mind if I join you?"

Startled, Terri nodded before she could think. The woman hopped up on the bar stool next to her and put her glass down.

"Thank you for the drink." It was the only thing Terri could think to say.

"My pleasure. I'm Arizona."

"Terri." Up close, Arizona was very attractive. Her chocolate eyes suggested that the blonde in her hair wasn't natural and her tan indicated that she enjoyed outdoor activities. Terri considered her unusual name, and a suspicion formed that this wasn't the only unusual thing about her.

They fell into conversation after that and it took a while for Terri to realize that Arizona was flirting with her. She kept trying to buy her drinks, which Terri refused after the second, and seemed very interested in why she would be at the bar by herself. Terri found herself divulging her breakup with Diane even though she'd had no intention of doing so. This only served to increase the flirting. Finally, after about an hour, Terri knew it was time to leave.

Arizona stood when she did and gave her another winning smile. "I hope we meet again," she said in a voice that sent a shiver down Terri's back.

"Yes." It was all Terri could think to say. As she left, she glanced back and saw Arizona in conversation with Mick. She wondered if Arizona was flirting with her as well. If she were, she wouldn't get far. Mick was fiercely devoted to the memory of her partner Angela and in five years had made no attempt to move on.

On the way home, it occurred to Terri what it meant if Arizona wasn't flirting with Mick. She dismissed the thought and concentrated on driving. She was much too old to be flirted with by a twenty-something, and far too old to respond if she were. However, part of her was flattered by the attention. It was more than Diane had shown her in the last three or four years.

When she got home, she went directly to her office, sat down at the computer and opened a new file. She planned on writing a sketch of Arizona, as she often did with people that she'd met. Her mind wandered as she wrote, touching on Arizona's looks and the casual way in which she flirted. After about half an hour, her attention returned to the computer and she looked at what she'd been writing.

As she read the story over, she was startled at the frank eroticism of it. It was like nothing she had written in the past fifteen years. Befuddled, she saved the story and got up to go to bed.

* * *

Terri pulled into the parking lot of About Face and put her car into park with an impatient shove. Carol had called her an hour before to let her know that Diane and her new lover were moving to Miami. It was unwelcome news, though at the same time brought a measure of comfort. Terri, tired of dealing with the dichotomy of emotions that Diane brought on, had decided that an evening chatting with Mick would be preferable to drinking a bottle of wine at home alone.

It was early on a Sunday night and as she expected the bar was almost empty. Mick was lounging on a stool in the corner watching the news when she came in. When she saw Terri, she stood up and waved.

"The usual?" Mick was fixing it before she could answer. "Any success in the writing?"

"Hell, no." Terri slid onto a stool. She accepted the drink and put a twenty on the bar. "Diane's moving to Miami."

"Oh." Mick shifted. "How do you feel about that?"

Terri drew her hand across her face. "That doesn't really matter, does it?" When Mick didn't answer, she added, "How do you think it feels?"

Mick was silent for a moment. "Depends on what mood you're in."

Terri sighed. "A confused one. Part of me is sad she's going, and the rest of me is glad to be rid of her."

"Then I expect you'll have more than one of these."

"Probably."

Terri and Mick chatted for about half an hour before the front door opened. Out of habit more than curiosity, Terri looked to see who it was. When she saw Arizona, her heart skipped a beat and she immediately wondered why. Arizona saw her and her face grew into a broad smile. She made a beeline for where Terri was sitting.

"Hi again. Mind if I sit here?" Terri gestured at the stool next to her, not answering. Arizona perched on it and ordered a drink. "May I buy you one too?" She gestured at Terri's empty glass. Terri nodded her assent and Mick, with a questioning look, went to make them. "I was hoping to see you again."

"I can't imagine why."

Arizona's grin was like a western sunset. "You're good looking, and interesting to talk to. What other reason could a woman need?" When Terri didn't answer, she added, "I like talking to you." Her eyes suggested that there was something more but Terri chose to ignore it.

"Well, you don't have to buy me drinks to talk to me.

"It's a habit. I won't offer again if you don't want me to." Arizona shrugged.

"It does feel a little strange to have someone your age buying me drinks," Terri admitted. Arizona laughed, but didn't reply. "I haven't seen you here before."

Arizona smiled. "I'm in town for a temporary assignment."

Terri raised an eyebrow. "What do you do?"

"I set up mainframes and do the programming to interface them with existing networks, primarily in the academic setting. I'm installing one at Stetson."

Terri's opinion of Arizona went up a few notches, as did her assessment of her age. "I teach English at the community college."

"That's cool. What kind of classes?"

"Literature and creative writing."

Arizona cocked her head. "Do you write too?"

"Yes." Terri knew what the next question would be. "And yes, I've been published; a long time ago."

"Anything I would have read?"

"I doubt it; it was in the early nineties." It occurred to Terri that Arizona was probably less than ten at the time. The thought made her uncomfortable.

Arizona took a long drink. "Why haven't you published anything since then? If that isn't rude to ask."

Terri sighed. "I was single then. Once Diane and I got together I just put all my energy into the relationship."

"This is the one you just broke up with?"

"Yes." Terri shut her eyes for a moment.

"You were together for a long time then." They chatted

for a while and then Arizona gestured at Mick with her empty glass. "Are you sure I can't buy you another one?"

Terri's mind told her to say no but something a little lower answered more loudly. "Why not?"

Arizona grinned and pointed at Terri's glass. Terri caught the confused look on Mick's face before she turned to make the drinks. "I'll be right back."

Terri watched the sway of Arizona's hips as she sauntered off toward the bathroom and blew out her breath. *What am I doing?*

"What the hell is going on?" Mick's voice drew her attention back to the bar.

"What do you mean? I just let her buy me a drink."

"Another drink," Mick corrected. "I'm glad you're getting back on the horse, but you should make sure the horse is over twenty-one first."

Terri frowned at her. "If she wasn't over twenty-one you wouldn't let her in here," she retorted. "And I'm not letting her pick me up, even if she's trying, which I doubt."

"Well by the way you're leaning toward her, you could have fooled me." Mick crossed her arms.

"Oh, my God." Terri rolled her eyes. "She was probably eight when Diane and I got together. I'm not about to rob the cradle."

"Well if you do, you're nuts. That little girl would kill you."

Terri started to reply before realizing that part of her was more than flattered by Arizona's attention. There was a tiny ache in the pit of her stomach that she hadn't felt in so long it had taken Mick's comment for her to recognize it. "You're right, she would. But I have to admit, being flirted with by a twenty-something is good for my ego."

Mick threw up her hands. "You *are* nuts."

"Maybe I am." Terri reached for her glass. "But don't worry; I'm leaving after this drink."

Mick made a disgusted noise and turned to serve someone across the bar. Terri glanced back toward the bathroom. Arizona was very good looking, appealing in a way that she couldn't quite understand. She wondered what she do if she actually did come on to her. She couldn't deny that her presence sent a thrill through her body.

Arizona returned and the two made small talk for another fifteen minutes or so; all the while, Terri's body sent out increasingly strong signals as to how attractive Arizona really was. Finally, she knew she had to leave before she did or said something she might regret. Arizona immediately offered to walk her out, and Terri caught Mick shaking her head when she said yes.

Upon reaching her sedan, she pulled out her keys and turned to Arizona. "Thank you for the drinks, and the company. I enjoyed it."

"My pleasure." Arizona's eyes searched hers. Terri met her gaze, not able to decipher its meaning. After a moment, and before Terri realized what was happening, Arizona leaned in and kissed her.

It wasn't a gentle kiss, rather questioning and expecting. Arizona's tongue traced a line along Terri's lips, slipping between when they parted. Terri's mind spun even as her mouth responded to Arizona's. Their tongues touched, retreated, and then touched again, moving against one another in a slow, languid dance.

When they finally parted, Terri looked at Arizona in shock. Desires long dormant, that she had thought would never return, thundered through her body *(How can a kiss make me feel like this?)* and coalesced in a throbbing pulse in the dominant part of her groin.

Arizona studied her as she tried to catch her breath. Just when she thought she had regained her reason, Arizona stepped forward, slid her arms around her waist, and kissed her again. This time her tongue was liquid fire; Terri tried (*I have to stop this*) to pull away until she realized that every sexual part of her being was ablaze with a hunger she hadn't felt in almost twenty years.

Arizona's mouth didn't leave hers as she took the keys from unresisting fingers. She pressed Terri against the side of the car as she unlocked the doors. Finally, she stepped away and studied her for a brief moment before reaching and opening the back door. She drew Terri to her and kissed her again as she maneuvered her onto the back seat.

"I shouldn't … I can't," Terri murmured as Arizona came on top of her. Her mind spun as Arizona kissed her once more, her tongue dancing in the wet warmth of Terri's mouth, her hands moving up her sides to cup her cheeks. Terri once again thought of pushing her away (*This is so wrong....*) but instead slid her arms around her waist and pulled her down more firmly against her.

Arizona made a sound of pleasure and pressed her hips against Terri's as her mouth moved to her neck. She bit her way down to her shoulder and then lifted away and brought her hands to the buttons of Terri's blouse. Quickly, the fabric fell away and once it was open Arizona pulled Terri's bra up.

"I knew they'd be wonderful," Arizona said in a thick voice as her hands found Terri's breasts. Terri arched her back and groaned when she felt the blonde's fingers pinch lightly against the hardness of her nipples, lifting them away from her body and rolling them. Arizona let them slide between her fingers and then reclaimed them, pinching slightly harder.

"Dear Lord," she gasped when Arizona dropped her head and drew a nipple into her mouth. Lightning charged through her body—"that feels"—and exploded—"so good…."—in the hard button between her thighs.

She didn't resist when Arizona brought her knees between her legs and spread them. She was gentle, making lazy strokes around Terri's nipple as she sucked it into her mouth and then hard as she bit down with enough force to draw a slight cry (*yes!*) and pummeled against the tip of her hardness with her tongue, pulling up and letting the nipple scrape through her teeth. She switched breasts and covered the first with her hand, her fingers replicating the movement of her mouth.

After a short time, Arizona stood up outside the car, reached down and unfastened Terri's belt and the button of her jeans. She wasn't entirely gentle as she pulled both pants and underwear down to Terri's knees. Terri stared up at her (*This can't be happening)* and she came back into the car, her fingers sliding into the tangled wetness of hair between Terri's thighs. When Arizona found her clitoris, Terri arched her back again and let out a long, impassioned groan.

"I wanted to do this the first time I saw you," Arizona said in a hungry voice, her fingers circling the hardened nub. Terri was unable to speak. "I wanted you like this." Her fingers slid down and found the source of the wetness that covered Terri's groin and inner thighs. Terri gasped as she felt two of them press inside her, gently but insistently. "Do you want this?"

"Yes." Terri couldn't believe the raw want that washed over her. Somewhere in the back of her mind came the thought that at any moment someone could come upon them. Even so, she wanted nothing more than for Arizona to take her. "Please."

Arizona began to move her hand, slowly at first and then with increasing speed and force as Terri's hips lifted against her. She leaned forward and captured a nipple once again between her teeth, lashing it with her tongue. Terri's hands sought some purchase, finally coming to the back of Arizona's head and drawing her mouth more firmly against her breast.

The sensation of Arizona's fingers thrusting into her (*Oh God, it's been so long)* was dizzying and Terri abandoned herself to the hungry pleasure. Before she realized it, she was trying to—"Yes!"—swallow a scream—"Arizona!"—as orgasm shattered through her. She heard the strangled guttural cry of her own voice as if it belonged to another person. Arizona held to her, thrusting into her as the orgasm rolled on. Finally, Terri closed her thighs and gasped, "No more."

Arizona held her hand still for a long moment and then pulled back, studying her. Terri fought for breath, her mind spinning (*Have I ever come that hard?*). Before the impact of what had happened had time to fully sink in, Arizona was unbuttoning her own jeans and coming on top of her again.

She caught Terri's wrist and guided her hand underneath the waistband of her boxer shorts. Terri felt the wetness between her thighs with a long groan, found Arizona's clit, and rubbed against it, relishing both the hardness and the way that Arizona's hips jerked forward against her fingers. Arizona pulled her T-shirt and sports bra up, bending over to offer Terri one of her nipples. Terri drew it into her mouth, eagerly suckling against it.

Arizona ground against her hand. "Fuck me," she ordered, arching her back to allow Terri to slide inside her, the slick walls of her heat pulling Terri's fingers in (*My God she's wet*) as she matched each thrust with her hips.

Finally, she pushed her jeans and boxers down past her knees and sat up, riding Terri's hand until, grabbing onto the headrests on either side of her, she let out a cry and came. Terri felt the wetness spill over her hand with a hungry pleasure (*Give me all of it!*) at having been responsible for it.

When Arizona had stopped shaking, she lifted up, backed out of the car, and pulled up her pants; panting, she looked down at Terri and grinned. The realization of what had just happened (*She's just a kid!*) began to sink in and Terri resituated her bra and reached for her jeans. Arizona watched her with a smile wreathing her lips. Sitting up, Terri buttoned up her blouse and crawled out of the car.

"Why?" It was the only thing she could think to say.

"You're gorgeous and you make me hot," Arizona replied simply. "And you obviously felt the same. What other reason did we need?"

Terri's knees went weak and she sat down. "I'm twice your age."

Arizona shrugged. "I like older women."

"I've never done anything like this in my life."

"Then you've been missing a lot." Arizona laughed. "You certainly seemed to like it. I'm not sure I've ever seen a woman come so hard."

Terri felt the blush shoot to her hairline. "I haven't had sex in three years," she mumbled.

Arizona stared at her. "You're kidding me." Embarrassed, Terri shook her head. "Holy shit. Well, that's a shame. I can do something about it."

"You just did." Terri looked at her curiously.

"I'd like to do it again," she said with a grin. "I'm in town for six weeks."

Terri's common sense returned. "I'm far too old for that sort of thing."

Arizona reached into her back pocket and pulled out her wallet. She extracted a business card and held it out. "I don't think so. Take my card, in case you change your mind. That's my cell phone."

Automatically, Terri took the card. Arizona smiled her one more time, turned around, and walked back toward the bar. Numbly, Terri watched her go. Finally, still feeling the tremors running through her body, she got up, closed the back door and opened the front. Sliding into the driver's seat, she stared across the parking lot.

"What did I just let happen?" she asked aloud sometime later. Knowing that no answer was forthcoming, she started the car and headed for home. As hard as she tried, her brain refused to process the implications of what happened. All she knew was that her body was sated in a way that it hadn't been for three years, probably longer.

Once she got home and the front door had closed behind her, it hit her that she had just had sex with a near stranger; a near stranger who was half her age, and in the back of her car on top of everything. She ran her hand over her face and groaned, but not from pleasure.

"Of all the dumb-ass things to do." she muttered as she crossed the living room to the bar.

After fixing a strong drink, she collapsed into her recliner and stared at the blank TV screen. Her friends would never believe this; not that she dared tell anyone. They would be certain she'd lost her mind and she wasn't sure she hadn't.

There was one certainty; she wouldn't call Arizona. The last thing she needed to do was get entangled with someone who obviously treated sex the same way most people treated dinner with a friend; enjoyable but not emotionally meaningful.

Terri thought back to the story she had written. How could she have known that it foreshadowed what had happened? She dropped her head back and sighed. It certainly wasn't the way she had envisioned her first sexual encounter after Diane, but it was and despite everything, she had thoroughly enjoyed it. In the morning, her senses would have returned to her and life would resume its normal, structured (*monotonous*) pace. She finished her drink and headed to shower before bed.

II.

Josie was on time, as usual; Terri let her in, offered her a drink—which she readily accepted—and led the way to the den. Once they were sitting down, Josie on the couch and Terri in the recliner, Josie leaned forward and studied her.

"Ready for the semester to start?"

Terri rolled her eyes. "What do you think?" she replied.

"At least you don't have introductory creative writing this year. Your students will have some sort of a grasp of story writing." Josie rolled her eyes right back at her.

"Well you try teaching Shakespeare to a bunch of freshmen before you think I'm too lucky."

"Why did they add that course anyway?" Josie shook her head. "Deconstructing Shakespeare; it still should be a 200 level course—at the very least."

"Ours is not to question why, ours is but to teach and die." Terri laughed.

Josie joined her. "You've been awfully quiet about your book," she said after the giggling stopped. "How's it going?"

Terri shrugged. "I finished another chapter."

"Finally."

"It took me a while to revise, and I'm still not completely happy with it." Terri looked away. "I can't believe it's so hard. You'd think this one would come easy."

Josie rolled her glass between her palms. "Are you sure you want to finish it?"

Terri considered her question. *Do I?* "I've started it; I

have to finish it, if for no other reason than to put closure on everything that's happened."

"Well let me read what you've got." Josie leaned back.

Terri sighed. "Alright, but don't expect Hemingway." She got up and went to the office, gathered the chapter together and returned to the living room, offering the sheaf of papers to her friend.

Josie put her drink down and took the manuscript, putting her glasses on. Terri sat back down and sipped at her drink, watching Josie's face as she read. After a few pages, Josie raised an eyebrow and glanced at her. She returned her gaze to the paper before her, her eyes scanning the words. She kept glancing up, until Terri knew something was wrong.

"What? It isn't that bad is it?"

Josie bit her lip. "I think you shuffled something in here you didn't mean to."

Terri furrowed her brow. "What do you mean?" Silently, Josie handed her two sheets of paper. Terri glanced at them and felt her face flame. "Oh, shit. Give me that."

Josie ignored her outstretched hand. "I want to see the end of it."

Terri closed her eyes and blew out her breath. "I was in a very strange mood when I wrote that," she responded weakly. "I never meant anyone to read it."

Josie pursed her lips. "Shut up and let me finish it."

Terri stood and went to fix herself another drink to hide her embarrassment. She returned to her chair, and stared at the floor until her friend put the papers down on the low table in front of her.

"Oh, my God," Josie said in a quiet voice. "I didn't know you could write like that."

"Please don't embarrass me any more than I already

am," Terri groaned.

Josie laughed. "I'm not trying to embarrass you. This is fabulous." Terri stared at her. "Yes, it needs some revision, but it's one of the best things I've seen you write years. It blows your old sex scenes out of the water."

"Do you really think so?" Terri returned slowly. "I wrote it off the cuff."

"If you can write this off the cuff, then I'd love to see what you could do with plotting. Where did it come from? Did you meet someone?"

Terri blushed, but for a different reason than her writing. "Sort of; she was just a girl at the bar. She bought me a drink."

"Getting hit on can bring this out? I can't wait to see what happens when you start dating." Josie chuckled.

"Who says I got hit on?" Terri asked archly. Josie simply held up the pages. "OK, so I got hit on."

"Do you think it will go anywhere?"

"No," Terri growled. "I'm not going to let myself get picked up in a bar." Inwardly she cringed, knowing she had done just that.

"Well, I think you should write more like this. If nothing else, it might help you get through the writer's block with the book." Josie studied her. "Though I don't suggest you bring anything like this to the writing group."

"Like I would."

Josie was silent for a moment. "I do know a group where it would fit perfectly."

"Where?" Terri raised an eyebrow at her.

"It's an online group. They call themselves Erotique." Josie blushed slightly and Terri stared at her.

"How do you know about it?" She raised the other eyebrow.

"I had a couple of wannabe Anaïs Nins this summer. I did some research to send them somewhere other than my class." She coughed. "Some of the stuff is really good."

Terri bit her lip. "I don't know," she said slowly. "I'm a little leery of joining a group of amateurs."

Josie laughed. "There are published authors on the list. Mostly short stories, and mostly erotica, but published just the same. It's all anonymous if you want it to be. I'll send you the link."

"I'll think about it."

The conversation turned to the coming semester and by the time Josie left, the writing group had all but vanished from Terri's mind. She gathered her papers together and went back to her office where she filed the story and promised herself that she would be more diligent in working on the book instead of things that she would never publish.

* * *

It was Wednesday, and Terri was sitting at the bar chatting with Mick, who was trying to pry information out of her about Arizona and failing. She had been there for about an hour when Arizona arrived. The sight of her sent an instant shock of arousal (*She really is good looking*) through Terri's body. She reminded herself that she was too old for meaningless flings, but her body appeared to be ignoring her.

Arizona didn't ask if she could sit down at this time, just slid onto the barstool next to Terri and grinned at her. Terri gave her a faint smile back and turned her attention to her glass. After placing her order, Arizona looked at her.

"You haven't called me."

"I told you I was too old for that sort of thing." Terri

tried to keep her face impassive.

"You're only too old if you let yourself think you are," Arizona returned. She was silent as Mick returned with her drink. "And from the way you responded to me I can tell you that you aren't too old," she continued after Mick had left.

Terri studied her. "You're pretty good at this, aren't you?"

Arizona shrugged. "What can I say, I like to have fun."

"Well, I'm not sure I'm ready for your version of fun. I just got out of a very long relationship, remember?"

"Then you aren't ready for an emotional commitment. You said you hadn't had sex in three years. Why not just enjoy getting some?" Arizona glanced at her. "You can't tell me I don't turn you on."

"Yes, you do. But there's a lot more involved than that." Terri had a sinking feeling that she was losing the fight.

"Like what?"

Terri opened her mouth, but nothing came out. She picked up her drink and took a long swallow, feeling Arizona's eyes on her the whole time.

"I just can't do it," she finally said weakly. As much as she hated to admit it, Arizona's forwardness was building a fire in her stomach that was getting harder to ignore with each passing minute.

"That's too bad." Arizona picked up her own glass. "I really liked what happened."

"So did I," Terri admitted slowly. When Arizona raised an eyebrow, she continued, "That doesn't mean I feel comfortable doing it again."

A few minutes passed in silence, until Terri knew that if she didn't leave she would end up in a position that she would regret the morning. She finished her drink and stood up; Arizona just looked at her as she said goodbye to Mick and then nodded when she told her to have a good night.

She was at her car when Arizona caught up with her. "Terri, wait."

Terri turned. "What?" Arizona studied her. Terri's heart started to pound and her nipples tingled into hardness. *Please don't kiss me. I don't think I could say no.*

When Arizona leaned in, the only thing Terri could do was close her eyes. Arizona's lips were soft, beckoning, and gentle. Terri couldn't help but respond as her mind played over what had happened after their last kiss.

"Please don't," she murmured when they parted, wanting nothing more than for her to.

"You don't sound very convincing," Arizona replied as she sought out Terri's lips again. She pressed her against the car, sliding her thigh between Terri's. Terri groaned. "You know you want me." Arizona's voice was a whisper as she traced the line of Terri's ear with her tongue.

Terri felt the rush of warmth between her legs and closed her eyes again. Arizona came back to her mouth, her hands sliding up to claim Terri's breasts. Terri rocked her hips forward against Arizona's thigh, sliding her arms around her waist.

She didn't stop her when Arizona unbuttoned the top of her jeans and slid her hand inside; as the young woman found her wetness, Terri gasped. Arizona began to rub against her clit as her tongue moved in Terri's mouth in a slow unhurried dance.

The sensation of Arizona's fingers on her sent waves of hunger through Terri's body. She groaned again as Arizona's lips came to her neck and she began to bite against her pulse, her fingers moving with more purpose. Terri's hips caught the rhythm and she pressed forward against

Arizona's hand.

Abruptly, Arizona stepped back (*Don't stop now. Oh, please, don't stop*) and pulled her hand out of Terri's pants. Aching with the nearness of climax, Terri watched as her companion brought her fingers to her mouth and licked the juices from them. A smile played along her lips.

"Call me." With that, she turned around and walked away.

Terri sagged against her car, feeling the pulsing want in her core. After a moment, she gathered herself together and shakily got into the driver's seat. She barely remembered driving home and collapsed across the sofa as soon as she got there, throwing an arm over her face. Her body still trembled with desire.

After lying there for what seemed like a long time, she got up and went to the office to try and write; it took her exactly eight minutes to decide that it was fruitless and she went back to the couch. She lay there a little while longer and then lifted her hand and traced it across her breast, feeling her nipple harden underneath her fingers.

She unfastened her blouse and shrugged it off, bringing her hand back up to circle across the hardened peak. She brought up her other hand and claimed its twin, rolling both between her fingers through the fabric of her bra. She felt the little jolts of electricity exploding (*Jesus!*) in her clit and pulled her bra off with an impatient motion.

Recapturing her nipples with her fingers, she let out a low guttural groan and arching her back slightly. The pulsing hunger between her legs continued to strengthen until she gave in; unfastening her jeans, she slid one hand beneath the band of her briefs. When her fingers found her wetness, she let out a louder moan and began to move against her clit as memories of Arizona thrusting into (*fucking*) her played through her mind. Her hips lifted off the couch in rhythm with her fingers as her other hand continued to pinch and roll at her nipples.

The tension began to grow in her body, and the images grew more graphic, sliding into fantasy of Arizona naked on top of her. She finally blew into orgasm with a strangled cry as wave after wave of pleasure broke over her body.

When she had come down, she stilled her fingers and let them rest, pressing lightly against her clit, fighting to catch her breath. *How long has it been since I did this; six months?* Arizona was getting to her, getting to that part of her she thought she'd lost through the years of monogamy and Diane's lessening sex drive.

Finally, she got up and kicked off her jeans, leaving them in a pile on the floor with her blouse and bra. She went into the bathroom and took a shower, then wrapped her robe around herself and returned to the office. Sinking down into her chair, she pulled out the story she had written and read over it. *It really isn't that bad.* It couldn't hurt to get some critiques from people who wrote the same sort of thing.

If nothing else, writing some erotica might help ease the aching need that she felt for Arizona's fingers. It took her half an hour to make the changes she thought the story needed, then, checking her email, she opened the message from Josie that she had ignored for the past two days and clicked on the link. It was a simple matter to sign up for the list, requiring only a valid e-mail address and a response to a follow-up message. She created a new account on her server with a nickname, just in case any of her students were also on the list, signed up and sent off an introduction.

Lying in bed later that night, she stared at the ceiling and wondered when it was that she had lost her hunger for the touch of a woman's fingers and lips; with the fading of those desires, she had also lost the will to write about such passion. If she couldn't feel the satisfaction of an exhausted afterglow there was nothing but the bitterness of its absence to stifle the words she once found to flow so freely.

Now, Arizona had rekindled that hunger, and it once again seemed ready to spill over onto the page. *Even if it's wrong, it feels so good to be desperate for someone again.* The thought disquieted her, and she rolled over, pulled a pillow over her head, and finally fell asleep.

When she checked her email the next evening, she found several messages from the list, including welcomes to her. They all said to jump right in and offer critiques or to post something of her own. There was a message from the list moderator with the appropriate etiquette for posting that she studied carefully before reading through the three stories that had been submitted for consideration. One was horrible. The next two had promise but required editing. Trying not to sound too academic, she posted critiques of all three and then posted the revised version of her own story.

After catching up with the rest of her e-mail, she went to the living room to watch TV. There was nothing on, so she returned to the office and pulled up the latest chapter of her book. She managed to eke out two pages before leaning back with a sigh and rubbing her temples. The phone rang. Picking up the handset, she turned it on and said hello.

"Glad to see you joined up," Josie said in greeting.

"You're on the list?"

Josie giggled. "Yes; like I said, some of it's really good. It might take a day or two for you to get responses. Not everyone checks or critiques until the weekend."

Terri paused, considering that Josie had never seemed like the sort of person who enjoyed erotica. "Do you write this stuff or just read it?"

"Don't forget it's *anonymous.* If I do write something you'll never know." She laughed. "No, I don't write it. I'll leave all the steamy stuff to you."

"It may just have been a fluke," Terri replied. "I haven't tried anything else."

"Please do." Josie sounded earnest. "You have a real flair for it."

"Are there many lesbians on this list?"

"A few; it's a minority, but it's there. You get good critiques from everyone though." Terri heard the sound of tapping. "I'm posting a critique of yours right now. I'll try not to make it too positive."

Terri chuckled. "Do you like the revisions?"

"Just wait until you read the critique."

"It won't be tonight. I'm worn out." Terri yawned.

"Well call me tomorrow," Josie said. "And pleasant dreams."

Terri hung up, saved her file, and went to bed, her thoughts on what Diane would've thought of the story. She would've hated it. She never had been the adventurous sort, preferring the tried and true. Arizona, on the other hand, would probably think it was too tame. With memories of Arizona dancing through her head, she finally fell asleep.

* * *

Terri got home from her department meeting annoyed and frustrated. There were new grading standards to be met and a host of other new rules that seem designed solely to make everyone's life miserable.

Pouring herself a drink, she kicked off her shoes and wandered into the office, sat down and pulled up her email program to check her messages. There were about twenty from the list including three regarding her story and one that looked like a response to one of her critiques. There was also a private message titled *RE: your story*.

She opened the list messages first. One was Josie's critique, which contained some good comments. One wasn't of much use, simply saying how much the poster had enjoyed it. The third was detailed and thorough, pointing out things that Terri couldn't believe she had missed. It was signed 'Misty Blue Eyes'.

Terri realized that the private message was from the same person. She opened it and scanned its contents. The author welcomed her as another lesbian and told her that she was impressed with the professionalism of the story. She noted that Terri's e-mail address told that she was from Central Florida and that she was from Saint Augustine. She also said that Terri had a solid grasp of editing from reading her critiques and wondered whether she was a teacher, as Misty herself was.

Terri hesitated in sending a reply, but in the end sent one off thanking the anonymous woman for her message and her critique and telling her she was from Daytona Beach and that yes, she was a teacher. She wasn't about to admit where, for fear that somehow it would come out that she was on the list.

She met Josie for an early dinner. They sat on the deck of a local seafood restaurant so that Josie could smoke and for a while discussed the department meeting. Then, finally, Terri brought up the list.

"I got a great critique from someone."

"Misty Blue Eyes," Josie replied. "I read it. She's usually dead on. She posts some great stuff too. Some of it gets kind of kinky, but you just can't stop reading it."

"She emailed me off list. She's from Saint Augustine, or

so she says." Terri paused to take a bite of her grouper. "She says she's a teacher."

Josie considered her words for a moment. "It wouldn't surprise me. She can be brutal in the grammar department. She does it in a nice way, but she's picky as hell."

"I noticed." Terri laughed. "I'll bet she's a bear in the classroom."

The conversation danced away and Terri didn't think about it again until she got home and checked her email. There was a message from Misty. When Terri opened it, she found that Misty wasn't at all surprised that she taught and hazarded that it was at a college level. She admitted that she taught at Flagler College and with a *lol* said that if any of her students ever found out she were gay, much less a writer of erotica, they would probably die. Terri thought it terribly trusting to give out so much information, but somehow it drew her in and made her curious to know more.

She replied that she also taught at the college level but that she wasn't comfortable revealing which college. She admitted that while she had written professionally, she was new to erotica. On a whim, she added that she was 50 and so was coming to it late.

She minimized her email program and started working on the book, trying to get more than two pages done. She had finished the first one when a ding told her she had a new e-mail. Assuming it was from the list, she didn't pay any mind, but after struggling through the second page, and eager for a break, she looked at the email.

It was from Misty. She told Terri that she was 45 and had come to writing to erotica only in the past couple of years. She had published a couple of short stories online and she laughed that she had gotten paid more for them than she had for a serious story in a print magazine. She told Terri that she was posting one of her stories that night and that she was looking forward to Terri's critique.

Terri sent a reply and then leaned back in her chair and stared at the picture over her desk. It was still early, and she didn't feel like being alone on a Friday night. She thought about calling one of her friends to go to a movie but for some reason she found herself going to the kitchen and pulling Arizona's card off the refrigerator. She looked at it for a long moment then picked up the phone.

Arizona was pleased to hear from her and they agreed to meet at About Face for drinks. Terri knew that more would be involved unless she could convince to Arizona that she was in fact too old for meaningless sex. She had to admit that Arizona raised desires in her that she hadn't felt in years, but was reticent to embrace them, feeling both guilty and confused that someone so young could arouse her so much.

As strong as she wanted to be, she knew that in the end, if she couldn't dissuade Arizona, she didn't feel guilty enough to say no. With a sigh, she went to change and then headed for the bar.

* * *

Arizona was waiting for her, and Terri had a suspicion she had already been there when she called. They took a booth in the corner and sipped their drinks for a few minutes, not saying much. Finally, Arizona reached over and covered Terri's hand with her own.

"I'm glad you called."

"I'm not sure why I did," Terri said quietly. "Despite everything, I'm still too old for you."

Arizona studied her. "So you came here to discourage

me?"

"The thought crossed my mind." Terri glanced away. "Something tells me you aren't dissuaded easily."

"I'm not."

"You left me in quite a state the other day." Terri blushed slightly. "It wasn't very nice."

Arizona chuckled. "That was the idea. Nice or not, it obviously worked. Did you go home and jack off?"

Startled, Terri stared at her for a second. The look on Arizona's face suggested she already knew the answer. Mutely, she nodded.

"I figured. If you hadn't, you'd have called me yesterday." Arizona grinned. "As long as you're a good girl, I promise not to leave you like that again."

Arizona's words sent a shiver of hunger through Terri's body. At the same time, they made her nervous. "I haven't said yes to anything yet."

With a shrug, Arizona leaned back and picked up her drink. She studied Terri with a stern expression. "If you didn't intend to say yes, then why did you dress like that?"

Terri realized that she had, indeed, dressed to be seduced. Her blouse had three buttons undone at the top and she had worn her best bra, the lace of which was just visible. She had picked the slacks which best flattered her hips and wore loafers that could easily be kicked off. Instead of her usual ponytail, she had pulled her hair back with combs.

"I like to look good," she responded weakly, knowing she was overdressed for the bar. She had seen the look on Mick's face when she walked in, that startled, 'What the hell are you doing?' look.

"You look good to me. Damn good as a matter of fact. I might have to buy you dinner before I fuck you senseless."

Terri screwed up her face. "I'm not particularly fond of that word." So why does hearing her say it make me want to beg for her to do just that?

Arizona shrugged again. "What else would you call it?" When Terri didn't answer, she smiled. "Actually, dinner sounds good."

Still fighting with herself, Terri nodded. "Sounds good to me too; just let me use the restroom first."

Arizona stood when she did. "I'll come with you."

There was no one else the bathroom when they went in. Both women chose their stalls and did what they needed to do but when Terri opened her door, Arizona was standing in front of her. She stepped inside, locking the door behind her.

"What are you doing?" Terri asked in shock.

In reply, Arizona pushed her up against the wall with a deep hungry kiss. Terri tensed and started to push her away, but when Arizona's tongue claimed hers, she found herself moaning instead.

Arizona pulled away from her body enough to unbutton her blouse the rest of the way. Her hands slid inside, claiming Terri's breasts over her bra. She insinuated a thigh between Terri's and pressed up against her groin. Terri's hips pressed back and she moved her hands to the back of Arizona's head, pulling her more deeply into the kiss.

After a minute or two, Arizona stepped back, her hands coming to the buckle of Terri's belt. Terri stopped her. "We're going to get caught," she said nervously.

Arizona grinned. "That's what makes it so arousing."

Surrendering, Terri let her unfasten the belt and the button of her slacks. Arizona slid her hand inside and found the wetness between Terri's thighs with a little groan. Terri tilted her head back as Arizona's fingers began to move against her, her hands grasping at Arizona's shoulders. Arizona kissed her again, pressing against her as she danced against her clit.

Terri felt the tension growing in her thighs and let out a low, hissing, "Oh, God." Just as she was sure that she was going to come, she heard the door of the bathroom open. Arizona instantly stilled her hand and Terri held her breath until whoever it was left again.

"We'd better not risk another interruption," Arizona said quietly, withdrawing her hand.

"But I'm so close," Terri gasped back. Arizona buttoned up her blouse, kissing her chest as she redid each button. "You promised you wouldn't leave me like this."

"After dinner I'll take care of this and more," Arizona replied, fastening Terri's slacks and belt. "I like the idea of you wanting me so desperately while we're eating."

"You're evil."

Arizona unlocked the door. "You won't be saying that in a couple of hours." She stepped out of the stall. "Come on, that friend of yours is probably wondering where we are."

Terri groaned, thinking of Mick, who had a remarkable talent of knowing exactly what was going on in her bar; she would certainly have noticed the two of them going into the bathroom and not coming out in a reasonable time. She followed Arizona back into the bar and sought Mick out, finding her busy on the other side of the bar serving a group of women. Terri blew out her breath, hoping she had been busy the whole time.

Trying to ignore the throbbing between her thighs, Terri looked at Arizona. "Where do you want to go for dinner?"

"I don't know; something light."

"I would just as soon forget dinner." Terri was shocked

when the words came out of her mouth.

Arizona grinned broadly. "Then we will. So, my place or yours?"

Terri blushed. The thought of doing the things with Arizona that she suspected she was going to do, in the bed that she and Diane had shared only a few months before, was too much. She knew that the next time a woman came to her apartment it would be for something meaningful, not what she knew Arizona had in mind. "Your place."

"Shall I drive? Or would you rather follow me?"

"I'll follow you."

With another grin, Arizona led the way out of the bar.

III.

Arizona was undressing Terri even as she was unlocking the door to her hotel room. Pushing inside, she kicked the door closed with her foot and finished unbuttoning Terri's blouse, sliding it off her shoulders. Her bra came off halfway to the bed and then Arizona was pressing her down with her body, kissing her hotly.

"God, I want you," Arizona breathed, standing up and undoing Terri's belt and slacks. Terri kicked out of her loafers and allowed Arizona to slide her pants down her legs, divesting her of the last of her clothing. She lay at last naked, and Arizona took in the length of her body with hungry eyes.

Terri watched as Arizona stripped, taking in the trim muscularity of her torso, her firm, slightly pendulous breasts and the tattoos on both of her upper arms. When Arizona's jeans and boxers hit the floor, Terri saw that she had been right to assume that Arizona wasn't a natural blonde. The hair at the join of her legs was dark and curled thickly in a neatly trimmed triangle.

Moving so that she lay fully on the bed, Terri waited to see what Arizona would do next. She didn't have to wait long before the younger woman came on top of her, nestling between her legs, her mouth seeking Terri's in a hungry, demanding kiss. Terri's lips parted beneath hers and she tasted the girl's tongue against her own in warm wet darkness.

Arizona began to move her hips against Terri's center, gyrating slowly but firmly as she pressed upward. Terri quickly caught the rhythm and they moved together as their lips crushed and their tongues battled. Terri couldn't believe the wanton desire she felt, couldn't believe (*Please, don't tease anymore*) how desperately she wanted to feel Arizona's fingers on her, in her.

As if reading her mind, Arizona slid off to the side and kissed her way down to Terri's breast, sucking the nipple into her mouth with a guttural sigh; Terri's back arched as thrills of pleasure raced through her body. Arizona claimed her other breast with her hand, taking the nipple between her fingers and squeezing lightly, releasing and squeezing again with a little more force.

She moved half on top of Terri's body and replaced her fingers with her mouth, drawing in the rigid nipple and scraping against it with her teeth. Terri groaned. Arizona's hand slid down her belly and into the tangle of her hair, her fingers exploring the depths and heights of her folds, dancing in her slick wetness.

"You get so wet," the blonde said in a slightly awed voice. "I could drown in you."

"I'm not like this," Terri gasped, trying to reassert her reason. "I don't need like this." She arched her back again as Arizona's finger slid across her clit and then returned to rub against it in a slow, insistent motion.

"Tell me what you want," Arizona ordered, nipping at Terri's breast. "What turns you on the most?"

The movement of her fingers made it hard for Terri to speak. Finally, she managed to get the words out. "Inside; three fingers."

With a low growl, Arizona did as she asked, sliding easily into her body. Terri bent her legs up, opening herself as Arizona began to press firmly into her. She pulled almost all the way out and then thrust back in. Terri shuddered. Arizona built the rhythm and the force of her hand as Terri lifted against her.

"Do you like this?" Arizona's voice was ragged. "Do you like to get fucked like this?"

Terri nodded her head quickly. "Yes." The word, which usually turned her off, sounded deep and vital; she couldn't imagine Arizona saying anything else.

"Tell me. Tell me you want me to keep doing it."

Terri brought her hands to her breasts, pinching at the nipples even harder than Arizona had. "Don't stop. God, don't stop."

Arizona's hand was practically slamming against her, her fingers driving inside with a force that made Terri dizzy; Diane had never been so rough, so intense. Terri couldn't believe that she hadn't come, couldn't believe that she wanted more.

She pinched and twisted her nipples as the rolling waves of pleasure thundered through her. At last, she felt the gathering and brought her knees up to her chest, drawing Arizona as far in as she could, and blew into an orgasm so strong that it sent dark spots dancing in front of her eyes.

Arizona's hand slowed and finally stopped, her fingers fully enclosed in Terri's still spasming well. Terri fought for breath, the heaving of her chest serving only to tighten her walls against Arizona's fingers, sending tiny aftershocks through her body. Withdrawing her hand, Arizona leaned forward and kissed her with surprising softness.

"How did you like that?" Arizona was breathing heavily as well.

"Oh. My. God."

Arizona grinned at her. "I never would have thought

you liked it that rough."

"Me either," Terri admitted slowly, her senses returning to her. "Diane never...." She trailed off, turning her head to stare at the wall. *Diane never....*

Arizona was silent. Finally, she lay down, resting her full weight on Terri's body, and nestled between her legs, with her hands sliding under Terri's arms to grasp her shoulders. Terri lifted her arms around Arizona's waist and they lay like that for a little while.

"I'm so wet for you I can hardly stand myself," Arizona finally said in a low voice.

"I'll do what I can." Terri felt uncomfortably awkward as she rolled Arizona on to her back, painfully aware that making love to Diane had become so rote that she wasn't sure she could do anything that Arizona wouldn't find boring.

She bent her head and drew one of Arizona's nipples into her mouth, her tongue flicking against it. Arizona shuddered when she brought her hand up and claimed the other breast, her fingers seeking out the twin of the hardened nub she held lightly between her teeth. Terri sensed that she wanted more and bit down harder. A low groan escaped Arizona's lips. She brought her hand up and pulled Terri's head more closely against her.

Terri kissed a hot wet line to the other nipple (*She tastes so different from Diane*) and repeated what she had done with the first. Arizona's hips rocked upward slightly, but when Terri slid her hand down into the tight curls covering her heat, she stopped her and came once again on top of her.

Terri could only lie in surprise as Arizona moved up her body, straddling her shoulders. She looked up, saw the silvery wetness between the young woman's thighs, and felt a shiver run through her body.

"I don't know if I can ... it's been so long since—"

"I'm sure you can figure it out," Arizona said as she lowered herself closer to Terri's face, grasping the headboard with both hands. "I want you to tongue me." It sounded like a command, and Terri didn't dare disobey.

Tentatively, she tilted her head, reached her tongue out, and ran it across Arizona's hair. She tasted the sweet thickness of the juice, digging in her memory for the last time her face had been between another woman's legs. She lifted her head and burrowed her tongue more deeply, just touching skin. The sensation awakened a hunger long buried and she brought her hands up to grasp Arizona's thighs and pulled her down, claiming her with her mouth.

Arizona exhaled a long 'yes' and tilted her hips down more firmly against Terri's face. Terri's tongue dipped into the source of her wetness and then slid upwards between her lips to press momentarily against her clitoris before sliding firmly off the tip. She remembered the joy of tasting a woman's arousal, something that Diane had hated both doing and having done.

It was with wonderment that she began to lap at Arizona's center, exploring the folds and valleys as though she were a virgin to the feelings and tastes. Quickly, she learned which motions caused Arizona to grind against her and those that made her gasp in pleasure. It didn't surprise her to find that biting against the swollen hardness of her clit made her shudder and beg for more and she pulled against it, sucking it into her mouth as her teeth closed down and her tongue lashed out. Arizona began writhing above her and Terri felt her clitoris hardening even more.

"Bite." The word was a guttural plea and Terri obeyed as Arizona thrust against her and came, the wetness flowing across Terri's chin and down her neck. She beat against the pulsing muscle with hard strokes of her tongue until Arizona tightened her thighs and pressed her hand against her forehead. Terri slowed and finally let her tongue still, released her grip on Arizona's legs and allowed her to lift herself away. Arizona collapsed beside her, gasping for air.

Terri wiped her hand across her face and turned on her side, studying Arizona's profile.

Finally, Arizona turned to face her. "How long did you say it's been?"

Terri blushed, the knowledge of how long it really had been only underscoring Arizona's youth. "A very long time," she finally managed to say.

Arizona laughed. "You have a good memory. Do you want something to drink?"

"What do you have?"

Arizona sat up and crossed her legs. "Bourbon and beer."

They both had a bourbon and water, sitting at the table under the room's one window. Terri rolled her glass between her palms, not quite able to meet Arizona's eyes. Finally, she lifted her gaze and looked into Arizona's face. "Thank you," she said simply.

Arizona shrugged. "As much of a pleasure for me."

"I still don't understand why...."

"I do. Stop questioning it."

"Why don't you have a girlfriend, someone your own age?"

Arizona stood up and paced a few steps. "I'm on the road twenty days out of thirty. It wouldn't be fair. Besides, girls my age don't know what they want yet. I don't want to give my heart away only to have it abandoned in six months, or a year."

"That seems kind of cynical." Terri studied Arizona's

back.

Arizona shrugged and turned around. "That's the way it is. What about you? Will you look for someone else?"

A pain hammered through Terri's heart. "I don't know," she responded slowly. "Twenty years is a long time to get over in a few months."

"Did you love her? At the end I mean."

Terri considered her words. Had she? "No; no, I don't think I did."

"Makes it easier to move on."

"I suppose it does." Why doesn't it feel that way?

They looked at each other silently for a while. Finally, Arizona ran a hand through her hair. "We've gotten into quite the serious discussion here."

"Yes."

"Well, let's lighten the mood. I hope you're ready for another round."

Terri grinned. "I believe I am."

Two hours later, Terri finally dragged herself out of Arizona's embrace and cried 'uncle'. They dressed in silence and had another drink.

"Do you still want dinner?"

Terri consulted her watch. "No. I should get home."

Arizona's face showed disappointment for just a moment, and then the leering grin reappeared. "I have to go to Tampa for a few days. Think of me while you're jacking off. I know you will be," she added when Terri started to protest. "Next time I'd like to see you jack off for me."

"Who says there'll be a next time?" Terri raised an eyebrow.

Arizona walked over to her, cupped her hand underneath Terri's chin and tilted her face upward. Her lips were quietly commanding. "There'll be a next time," she whispered before straightening up. "Give me your number. I'll call you when I get back."

Against her better judgment, Terri wrote her cell phone number on the hotel notepad. "I can't guarantee this will happen again. I'm not completely comfortable with it."

Arizona's face told her that she didn't believe her, but she said, "I hope it does."

After finishing her drink, Terri escaped to her car. Putting both hands on the steering wheel, she blew out her breath and wondered why her self-control kept abandoning her when she was around Arizona. Her mind refused to supply an answer and she started the car and headed home.

* * *

Terri paced her apartment with a drink in her hand. She could still smell Arizona on her face and the scent kept tickling at her clit but she didn't want to take a shower yet, not willing to relinquish the pleasurable sensations lingering in her body.

Even in the early years, Diane hadn't been particularly adventurous in their lovemaking and Terri hadn't pushed the issue, being so smitten that the pleasure she received from even the mundane couplings was more than satisfying. Diane had never had much of a sex drive and over the years, they fell asleep in the warm afterglow less and less. It happened so slowly that Terri never really missed it.

And now Arizona had sparked that fire and it was rapidly growing into an inferno. As much as she wanted to deny it, she knew that when Arizona returned she would willingly go into her arms again. There was no emotional attraction at all; something that confused and bothered her, but at the same time made what was happening all the more exciting.

Terri sipped at her drink and paced some more. It made no sense that she could have such a deep want for someone so soon after Diane had left, but it was there and she couldn't make herself question it. Her mind was filled with situations in which she could find herself with Arizona, situations that she had never dreamed of with Diane.

With a sigh, she gave into the knowledge that she was still wet and wondered what to do about it. She could shower and go to bed, and take care of it herself. That was the logical thing to do. Somehow, she knew that it wouldn't be satisfying; she felt the need to express the feelings that trembled through her body.

She wandered into the office and sat down at her computer, idly checking her mail. The story that Misty had promised was posted but she had a suspicion that reading it would only serve to put her into a worse state than she already was. She pulled up a blank document in her word processor and stared at the white page for a while before starting to type.

It took her an hour to complete the story; when she was done, she leaned back and reread it. Short, sweet, and to the point, it was a vignette between two women that raged with simmering sensuality. Sighing, she printed it out and set it to the side so that she could revise it in the morning. It seemed that lately sex captured her interest more than her novel's storyline of waning interest and deception.

Deciding that she couldn't be in much worse of a state than she already was, she returned to her e-mail and pulled up Misty's story. The first paragraph had her sweating; by the time she was finished reading, she was ready to slide her fingers between her thighs right where she was sitting.

It was stunningly erotic, the descriptions flowing

liquidly from seduction to satisfaction. Her body trembling worse than it had been before, she sent off a quick note to Misty telling her how wonderful the story was and that she would do a critique as soon as her hormones had settled down. It wasn't until she had already sent it that she realized what she had typed. Running a hand across her face, she decided that a shower and bed were the best things for her.

Standing under the hot water, she gave into the sensations running through her body and dropped her fingers between her legs (*How can I still be so turned on?)* rubbing her clit as her other hand—"Yes!"—found a nipple. She leaned against the wall of the shower and relished the movements until the ripening heat was too much to stand; she sank down into the tub and let the orgasm overtake her.

As she toweled off, it occurred to her that she had come more in the last week and she had in the last two years. Shaking her head, she went to the bedroom and crawled under the covers, not bothering with the t-shirt and sleep pants she normally wore. The sheets were soft against her naked skin and she fell asleep imagining that she was one of the women in Misty's story, and for some strange reason that Misty was the other.

An e-mail from Misty greeted her the next morning when she took her cup of coffee into the office. She could almost hear the laughing tones in her voice as she wrote that she was glad Terri had enjoyed her story so much. She shared more information about herself, including that she was single (as if Terri couldn't tell from her story, she laughed).

Terri replied that she was single too, and mentioned the amount of time that she and Diane had been together. She shared a little more about herself as well and closed by saying that she was going to do a critique and then possibly post another story of hers.

After a flurry of emails back and forth during the day, Misty finally suggested that they meet for drinks the next evening. Terri found herself agreeing. As she signed off and went to bed, she wondered what had come over her. Between Arizona and agreeing to drinks with a stranger she had met online, she was definitely not behaving in the careful, conservative manner that had defined her for so many years. Could Diane have had that much of an influence over her?

Refusing to let the questions keep her awake, she snuggled under the covers and cleared her mind.

* * *

"You're nervous is a cat," Mick observed. "Waiting for Arizona?"

"Why would you say that?"

Mick laughed. "Oh, please. You think I didn't notice the other night?"

Terri's face flamed. "I was hoping you hadn't."

"You're a big girl." Mick shrugged. "So are you waiting for her not?"

"No. I'm meeting someone else." Terri poked at her drink. She had told Marie where she would be sitting, and what she would be wearing, but she still wondered whether she would even show up, and what they would talk about if she did.

Mick made a noise in the back of her throat. "I hope this one is older."

"It isn't like that. She's a member of a writing group I belong to."

Mick rolled her eyes, before turning to tend to someone on the other side of the bar. Terri glanced at her watch. *She said she'd be here about eight. Its 8:05. I wonder if she's going to show.* She poked at her drink some more.

A few minutes later, she sensed someone come up beside her.

"You must be Terri."

Terri turned and looked into green eyes that seemed to glow in the dimness of the bar. She caught her breath; Marie was beautiful. Curly hair, burnished red, fell to her shoulders. Her face was oval and open, her lips full and inviting. The sharp sting of arousal hardened Terri's nipples almost instantly; she forced herself to exhale.

"And you must be Marie." She almost cringed when she realized how weak her voice sounded.

"I certainly hope so; otherwise I have the wrong driver's license," Marie responded wryly. "You look a little different than I expected."

Terri coughed. "So do you."

"Just goes to show you can't judge someone by their writing." She sank onto the barstool next Terri and gestured at Mick. "I haven't been in here in a while."

Terri just nodded, and caught the look that Mick threw her as she came over to take Marie's order; she asked for a Corona with lime.

"Are you ready for the semester to start?" She was desperate to take her attention away from what she figured was a rather obvious study of Marie's chest.

Marie grinned at her. "Are we ever *actually* ready for that?"

"I suppose not," Terri admitted. "It's going to cut into my writing time significantly."

"Yes. You wrote *A Kiss of Honey*, didn't you?"

Startled, Terri stared at her. "You've heard of it?"

"I own a copy. I also read *Surrender to Me*. You've improved over the years. Not that you were bad before," Marie added hastily when Terri raised an eyebrow, "but your sex scenes certainly have more zing."

"It's been a long time since I was published."

"Are you working on anything now? Or are you concentrating on the short erotica?"

Terri blushed. "I've only just started writing that. I'm in the middle of a book. It's just giving me fits, though. I'm about ready to kill-file the whole thing."

Marie took a sip of her beer. "Is it another romance?"

"No. It's a ... it's a story about struggle and the deterioration of a relationship."

"Sounds kind of heavy. I take it it's not going as smoothly as you'd like."

"No, it's not." Terri sighed. "I started it before my partner left. Now it seems kind of pointless, but I'm half way through it and I hate to give up that much work."

Marie gave her a look that suggested that she had seen right through the comment into the core of the truth; that Terri was hanging onto the story as a way of keeping Diane near her. *But she can't possibly know that.*

"Just have to stick it out to the end, eh?"

"I have so many hours into it now that I feel like I have to finish it just on the principle. It's funny; when I was writing romances, I could finish a book in about three months. This one's taken me a year and at the rate I'm going it's going to take me another year to get finished."

"Is it about your partner?"

"Partially," Terri admitted. "We were having problems for a while before we split."

"You were together for a long time, weren't you?"

When Terri flushed, she looked slightly apologetic. "I'm sorry, none of my business."

"It's OK; yes we were. Twenty years. How about you?"

Marie shrugged before smiling. "My longest was ten years. I swore off of them after that. I prefer to be footloose and fancy free."

For just a moment Terri wondered if footloose and fancy free to Marie involved the college-aged women on her campus. *Don't be ridiculous; just because you're robbing the cradle doesn't mean everyone is.* "Have you written any book length fiction?"

"No; nonfiction has been my specialty. I wrote a textbook on lesser known women poets of the late nineteenth century a few years back. As far as fiction goes it's always been short stories and a novella or two."

The conversation turned to literature and what both women considered the sad state of its place in the modern college education. After Terri's second drink, it struck her that Marie hadn't finished half her beer.

"You don't really drink, do you?"

Marie's lips curled into a smile. "No, not really."

"We can go somewhere else if you'd prefer." Terri felt embarrassed for not having noticed sooner.

"That's quite all right." Marie waved a hand in dismissal. "I draw inspiration from everyone around me. This is a different setting to get some characters from."

I wonder what she'd think about Arizona. "You mentioned that you had submitted some stories on line. Are their acceptance standards the same as print magazines?"

"They can be."

"I'd like to submit, but of course it would be under a pen name. I can't imagine what would happen if one of my students found out I wrote that kind of thing."

Terri studied Marie's face in the dimness of the bar. She was a very striking woman, looking younger than her 45 years. She was comfortably dressed in a pair of jeans and a long sleeve Oxford shirt that fell over her ample breasts (*I could get lost in that cleavage*) with a softness that suggested it had been well worn. The tingling in her breasts, which she had managed to put aside, returned almost painfully.

Diane had been black haired and dark skinned, her Italian background clearly evident in her features and her attitude. That darkness is what had originally drawn Terri in; she'd found Diane mysterious and intriguing. She had aged well, and the physical attraction had never gone away. At least for Terri it hadn't. As soon as Diane hit menopause, her interest in sex had vanished completely.

Marie was very different; of obviously Irish descent, her skin was light and freckled. She had high cheekbones and a strong jaw. Everything the opposite of Diane, and yet as attractive.

"...and so of course, in order to do research, I looked up all the sites I could find."

Terri blinked several times and drew her attention back to the Marie's words.

"You weren't paying a bit of attention to what I was saying, were you?"

Terri's blush burned her cheeks. "I'm sorry," she mumbled.

Marie laughed. "It's OK. I get bored listening to myself sometimes."

"I wasn't the least bit bored," Terri replied. "I just got to thinking about...."

"What was her name?"

"Diane."

"What happened, if you don't mind my asking? You can

always tell me to shut up."

The heat in Terri's cheeks intensified. "She found someone else."

"Oh." Marie fell silent.

Terri shrugged. "Like I said; things hadn't been good for a while."

"Whoever it was must have been something to take her away from you."

When Terri met her gaze, Marie was blushing as well. "I don't know; I never met her."

Neither spoke while they finished their drinks. Terri became painfully aware during the silence of the rise and fall of Marie's chest. *What has gotten into you?* She couldn't deny that she found Marie very attractive. *Your hormones have been in overdrive for the last week.*

When they started talking again, it was about writing. After about an hour, Terri suggested dinner, which Marie politely declined, and they sat for another pleasantly comfortable twenty minutes before Marie excused herself saying that she wanted to get some writing done before bed.

Terri, certain that she had put Marie off in some way, (*Why would you care?*) stood when she did and smiled. "I had a very good time. Thanks for meeting with me."

Marie's smile was slow and seductive, although Terri was relatively sure it wasn't intended that way. "I think meeting you is the best thing that's happened to me this summer. I look forward to reading some more of your work. Drop me an e-mail when you get home."

Terri agreed and watched Marie's hips carry her out of the bar. Once the door had closed behind her, she sank back down and gestured for another drink.

"You shouldn't have another one of these," Mick commented as she set the glass down. "This makes four."

"Don't worry; I'm going home after this. I'm just processing."

Mick followed her gaze to the door. "She's quite the looker."

"Yes, she is. But I'm not interested."

"Right; you've got your little baby dyke to play with."

Terri rolled her eyes. "Nothing's going to come of that. I doubt she'll even call me when she gets back from Tampa."

"I still think that little girl will kill you."

Quite possibly. "I have to admit it's a little thrilling to have someone chasing me like that."

"You're incorrigible." Mick leaned against the counter. "I never knew you were such a dirty old woman."

Terri stuck out her tongue. "I'm just rediscovering that sex can be fun. You can't tell me that you've been celibate for the last five years."

Mick looked faintly abashed. "Well, no, I haven't been. But at least mine weren't in diapers during the Reagan years."

"Like I said; nothing's going to come of it. I told her I wasn't comfortable with the way things were going." She wasn't sure what she would do if Arizona did call. Their relationship (*If that's what you could call it*) was simply untenable.

Arizona had circumvented her reason long enough; it was time for Terri put an end to it. Regardless of how good the sex was, Arizona was too young for her, and would hurt her—physically, at least—if things continued the way they were.

Finishing her drink, Terri said good night to Mick and went home. As she crawled into bed, her thoughts turned to the last story she had read of Marie's. Now, having met her, she found it even easier to place them both in the roles of those characters. She wondered what Marie would think if she knew.

Somehow, the thought of finding out made her shiver. Marie hadn't done or said anything to make Terri think her interest was returned, and she worried that letting on how attractive she thought Marie was would jeopardize what promised to be a good friendship.

With the groan, she pulled a pillow over her face. *Terri McKenzie, you'd better pull yourself together before your hormones get you in way over your head.* With that stern warning to herself, she closed her eyes.

* * *

They stopped by the bar after the movie. It was the fourth time they had been out in the previous two weeks and Terri knew that the time was coming when she and Marie would have to make a decision; sleep together or just remain friends.

The pair had been there for perhaps thirty minutes when the door opened and Arizona strolled in. Terri's heart stopped beating for a second and then resumed at a rapid pace. The last thing she wanted was for Arizona and Marie to meet. Arizona would most likely make a comment that would give Marie the wrong impression about her.

Arizona spotted her almost immediately and made a beeline for where the two women sat.

"Well, hello Terri," she said in her seductive voice.

"Hi," Terri responded weakly.

"This a friend of yours?" Arizona looked Marie up and down before returning her gaze to Terri's face.

"Yes. This is Marie. Marie, this is Arizona, a … friend of mine."

Marie studied Arizona for a long moment before turning a questioning eye to Terri, who blushed.

"Nice to meet you," Marie said finally. "Won't you join us?"

"I'd love to." Arizona pulled up a barstool and sat down. "Can I buy you ladies a drink?"

Terri started to demur but Marie beat her to the punch. "Certainly." She smiled.

Defeated, Terri accepted the drink that Mick handed her with an embarrassed smile.

"I can only have one more and I really should leave," Marie commented. "I have a meeting in the morning."

"Do you have to go so early?" Arizona's voice was innocent. "If I'm interrupting something…."

"No, I really do have to go." They finished their drinks, making small talk as Terri tried desperately to keep the conversation away from anything that might give Arizona an opening to make a revealing comment.

Finally, Marie took her leave, kissing Terri on the cheek and whispering a good night in her ear that left her aching.

Once she was gone, Arizona turned to her with a wry grin. "She's good looking."

"Yes, she is."

"Do you think she'd like to join us?" Arizona gave her a look that boded no good.

"What!? No! I wouldn't even ask her." The thought sent an unexpected chill down Terri's spine.

"Relax; I was just kidding with you."

"It's hard to tell with you sometimes." Terri relaxed, somewhat. She was still tensed with the knowledge that she most likely wouldn't be leaving alone. Despite Marie's nearness only a short time before, the thought of being with Arizona brought a heat that she would have thought impossible a few weeks before.

"So, do you remember what I said last time we were together?" Arizona finished her drink and gestured for another.

"Not really."

Arizona leaned over to her as Mick brought the drink. "I said I wanted you to jack off for me when I got back."

Terri went bright red almost instantly. *Oh, God....* Mick gave her a strange look then went back to the other side of the bar.

"I can't wait to watch you," Arizona continued almost conversationally. "I don't think I can wait until we get back to the hotel."

Please not the car. "Where would you like to go, then? And that wasn't a yes, by the way." *You know you're turned on, why deny it?*

Arizona grinned. "Yes, it was. Finish your drink."

Terri found it impossible to deny the command. When she was through, Arizona got up and led her out the back door.

Instead of the car, however, she led the way to a path in the woods at the back of the parking lot. When Terri hesitated, she took her hand and pulled gently. "Come on, it's safe."

The path was short and ended at the chain link fence that was supposed to keep people out of the park that ran beside the bar. There was a hole in the fence, and Arizona ducked through it.

"Come on," she repeated, holding out her hand again.

Terri drew in a deep breath, bit her lip, and followed. On the other side, Arizona led her out of the trees and onto the grass, stopping by a picnic table. She pulled Terri to her and pressed her lips against hers in a hot, passionate kiss.

Terri melted beneath her mouth, her lips parting as Arizona's tongue insinuated itself inside.

Their tongues touched, danced, and then Arizona pulled away. She sank down on the table, bringing Terri with her. It was cool, but not uncomfortable. Without a word, Arizona started to unfasten the buttons of Terri's blouse. Acquiescent, Terri sat still as she pulled open the fabric and her hands slid around Terri's back to unfasten her bra.

The cool air hit Terri's nipples and they tingled into hardness. Arizona finished pulling off her top before her hands came to her breasts. Her fingers found Terri's nipples and pinched lightly at them. Still without speaking, Arizona leaned in and kissed her again, and then moved her mouth down and sucked a nipple into her mouth, rolling the other between thumb and forefinger.

Terri arched her back, pressing against Arizona's lips. Arizona suckled at her breast before kissing a hot, wet line to the other one, covering the first with her palm. Terri felt the rush of wetness between her thighs with guilty pleasure.

Too soon, Arizona sat back.

"Unfasten your pants," she ordered. Startled, Terri complied. Arizona pulled them down and grinned. "Expecting to get some?" Terri had worn a pair of lace panties, not because she was expecting Marie to see them, but because ... *Because it made you hot thinking she might.*

"No." Terri's breath came raggedly, and she cursed inwardly at how quickly Arizona could bring her to a panting, quivering need.

Arizona pulled the underwear off and then ran her fingers up the insides of Terri's thighs and brushed across the curly hair at their join. "Jack off for me."

Startled, Terri stared at her and Arizona looked back, calmly. Terri found herself unable to say no.

She dropped her hand between her legs and found her swollen clit. Feeling very self-conscious, she began to move her fingers across it, the sensations shooting up her body and exploding in her nipples. Arizona reached out and closed her fingers around those hardened buds.

Terri's hips caught the rhythm of her fingers and she closed her eyes. *Yes, Marie, there.* She knew it was Arizona at her breast, but her mind too easily supplied another face.

Her embarrassment faded as the tension in her clit grew. Finally, she blew—"oh, God!"—into a hard—"Ari-"—rolling—"zona!"—orgasm that shook her body—*Marie!*—with its intensity.

When she had come down, she opened her eyes and found Arizona studying her with a bemused expression.

"You were thinking about her, weren't you?"

"Yes," Terri admitted.

To her surprise, Arizona laughed. "Good. You deserve someone nice."

"But you know if I sleep with her, I can't...."

"Sleep with me?" Arizona finished. "I know. And part of me is sad about that. But I saw the passion you had hidden inside, and I set out to free it. I've done that, and now it's time for you to move on."

Terri realized this was their goodbye. To her surprise, she felt a sense of loss. "You won't call me, will you?" It wasn't a question.

"No." Arizona was silent for a moment, her face pensive. Then she smiled again. "I'm almost done here anyway. Time to move on to another project."

It took Terri a moment to realize she was talking about work. "I'll ... miss you, in a way."

"No, you won't," Arizona replied. "You'll be so involved with Marie you won't miss anything. Except her arms when she isn't there."

Terri dressed in silence and the pair walked back to the parking lot. Standing beside her car, Terri leaned over and kissed Arizona gently. "Thank you."

"My pleasure." Then Arizona was gone, strolling back into the bar as though nothing had ever happened between them.

Terri stood there for a long time, and then got into her car and pulled out her cell phone.

"Marie? How'd you like to come to dinner at my place tomorrow night?"

BOOKS BY CAPE WINDS PRESS
available in print and Kindle format

A Wild Sea (Rebecca Montague)

Katherine thought she was coming to Smith Island to say goodbye to the personal ghosts that haunted the place, but some things refuse to go quietly ...

Allergic Reaction (Leslie Adams)

The last place police Detective Porter Sienna wanted to investigate a murder was the upper class neighborhood where she grew up...

Barnfire (Rebecca Montague)

Elizabeth Casey wasn't looking for romance when she came to spend the summer on her aunt and uncle's farm in rural Pennsylvania. She certainly didn't expect to find it in the arms of a reclusive local painter old enough to be her mother ...

Tahoma (M. Broughton Boone)

The year is 1883, the place is the Washington Territory and Agnes Farwell still mourns the death of her father less than a year before. All she wants is the house her father had promised her, a house whose shell sits as empty as her heart ...

www.ingramcontent.com/pod-product-compliance
Lightning Source LLC
La Vergne TN
LVHW020627100826
845148LV00012B/2083

* 9 7 8 1 5 8 9 7 2 0 0 7 7 *